# HELL
# IN HIS
# HOLSTERS

**Center Point
Large Print**

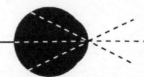

**This Large Print Book carries the
Seal of Approval of N.A.V.H.**

# HELL
# IN HIS
# HOLSTERS

## Charles N. Heckelmann

CENTER POINT LARGE PRINT
THORNDIKE, MAINE

This Center Point Large Print edition
is published in the year 2012 by arrangement with
Golden West Literary Agency.

Copyright © 1952 by Charles N. Heckelmann.
Copyright © 1953 by Charles N. Heckelmann
in the British Commonwealth.
Copyright © renewed 1980 by Charles N. Heckelmann.

The text of this Large Print edition is unabridged.
In other aspects, this book may vary
from the original edition.
Printed in the United States of America
on permanent paper.
Set in 16-point Times New Roman type.

ISBN: 978-1-61173-424-9

Library of Congress Cataloging-in-Publication Data

Heckelmann, Charles N. (Charles Newman), 1913–2005.
Hell in his holsters / Charles N. Heckelmann. — Large print ed.
p. cm. — (Center Point large print edition)
ISBN 978-1-61173-424-9 (lib. bdg. : alk. paper)
1. Large type books. I. Title.
PS3515.E1857H43 2012
813'.54—dc23
2012004305

# TO MY WIFE

# HELL
# IN HIS
# HOLSTERS

# One

THE Chevron trail herd came over the ridge in a wide, loosely bunched line. They were prime Herefords, their heavy frames amply covered with fat after long months of feeding on Wyoming grass.

Well out in front of the herd, riding point, a position he had maintained during the entire fifty-mile trip from the Chevron ranch in Capricorn, Dave Flood halted his roan gelding at the foot of the yonder slope to gaze across the wide expanse of flats that terminated in the railhead town of Blue Mesa.

Directly to the east the grass-covered prairie extended for a distance of several miles. There were just two breaks in the prairie. The first was Little Teton Creek, which thrust a narrow blade of silvery brilliance across the land.

The second, beyond the creek, was the town itself, which from Dave Flood's position looked doll-like and unreal.

Flood pulled his attention back to the Chevron herd, then slowly lifted his arm in a forward motion to the two punchers riding swing. Immediately the two rannies lifted their voices in a shrill "hi-yi" and sent the steers down the slope. The animals needed no urging, for they had already scented the cool creek water, and moved forward in a shambling run. The flank riders sped up the line, pressing the bunched cows into a tight, orderly phalanx.

"Hold them down, Hoot!" Flood yelled before turning his roan gelding to ride on.

The puncher on the left flank rode in closer to the steers, further tightening the line. The man posted on the opposite flank followed the same maneuver. With water in view there was danger that the thirsty animals would stampede into the creek and drink too heavily while still hot from the long day's march.

With Flood patrolling back and forth across the point of the herd the animals were slowed down and finally forced to mill. The drag rider, his neckerchief still covering his mouth and nose, cantered up and lent a quick hand as the Chevron beef was halted a quarter mile from the creek.

At the same time a girl on a pinto pony joined the left flanker in monitoring the outer ranks of the milling steers. Flood called to the man near her.

"Hoot, come over a minute."

Hoot Ellison swung his horse around and quickly sped to Flood's side. The two men were a study in contrasts. Ellison was slender and of medium height. He had narrow shoulders and a ruddy face that was thin without being gaunt. His gray-green eyes were alert and steady and his hair was thick and light brown in color. Even-tempered and intensely loyal, he was one of the best-liked hands on the Chevron ranch.

Flood, on the other hand, was a taciturn, humorless man. Rangy, six feet tall and wide-shouldered, he carried most of his weight in his chest, his upper arms, and his solid muscular legs. Like most men of the range, his waist was trim, hammered down by long hours spent in the saddle. He had ice-blue eyes, now thinly drawn together under his warped hatbrim by the glittering wash of sunlight. He was dressed in somber black, from his dusty Stetson to the open-necked shirt and tight-fitting pants tucked into worn half-boots. There was a single gun on his right hip. It was a plain affair, cedar-handled but well-oiled and swinging free in an open-flap holster.

As the glances of the two men met, Ellison said, "You going on into town to see Neil Gray?"

"Yeah," replied Flood. His keen eyes scanned the herd. "Better start watering them, then bring them back and bed them down along here. When I find Gray I'll bring him back here to have a look at the critters."

He started off at a trot, but had traversed only a few rods when the pounding of hoofs behind him brought him sharply around in his saddle.

"Wait for me, Dave," said Nell Raines as she brought her pinto up beside the big roan.

"Sorry, Nell. I should have realized you

wouldn't want to waste any time going in to Blue Mesa so you can get cleaned up."

Nell Raines, niece of Big Tom Raines, owner of the Chevron outfit, smiled. "A hotel bed, even if it is one of those creaking beds in the Tumbleweed Hotel, will feel good after two nights sleeping with a bunch of cows."

"You wanted to come along," Flood reminded her.

"Sure I did," Nell said. "And you've got to admit I saved you an extra hand."

There was a soft loveliness in Nell's high-cheeked, well-tanned features. The eyes were a clear deep blue behind dark lashes. Her hair was blond and wavy and carefully imprisoned by the brim of a fawn-gray sombrero with a thin chin cord that molded the firm, strong curve of her jaw. Her nose was small and straight, the nostrils just faintly flared. Her lips were long and full and made for smiling, but they had a way of going still that warned of hidden wells of strength in her.

Just to look at Nell stirred Flood's senses. He'd never given much thought to women in his travels through the West until he'd come to the Chevron. But Nell with her rich beauty, her quick competence, her ability to do a man's work in a man's world had gotten inside him. On the trail she had carried off her duties as capably as any cowpuncher. She could rope and ride extremely well, and she could handle the nickel-plated .38 revolver she wore in the worn holster snugged against her hip.

It was a nice hip, Flood reflected, his eyes slanting along the proud, firmly molded contours of her body. Even the faded blue work shirt she wore could not hide the full sweep of her taut young breasts. With her body so close to his Flood had to stifle the desire to take Nell in his arms. He'd done it only once during his tenure at the Chevron, but it was something he would long remember—the warm circle of her arms around his neck, the solid thrust of her breasts as he pulled her against him, and the torrid rush of feeling that had raced through him at the touch of her hot, seeking mouth.

Now he grinned faintly, wondering if the tumult inside him was reflected in his eyes. "Come along, Nell. I want Gray to see your uncle's beef before dark." They cut diagonally toward Little Teton Creek, finally following its southerly course until they reached a muddy ford. They splashed through the shallows and continued on to the main street.

Flood and Nell made their way directly to the Tumbleweed Hotel. Three horses stood hipshot at the hitching rail. Farther on, at the Latigo Saloon, a dozen more horses announced the fact that the day had been hot and business was good.

Flood swung down from the roan and lifted his

arms to assist Nell from the saddle. For a moment her body was soft and pliant against him and her face was very near. Then she gave him a fleeting smile and pulled away.

"Meet me here for supper around six," she said.

Flood nodded. "All right." Then he glanced past Nell as the hotel steps vibrated to the passage of a heavy man. Quickly he called out a greeting. "Neil, you're just the man I'm looking for."

Neil Gray, a partner in the Kansas City packing firm of Gray and Phillips, came on down the steps and removed his hat out of deference to Nell.

"Howdy, Dave," he murmured in a deep, measured voice. "It's nice to see you. And you, too, Miss Raines."

Nell acknowledged Gray's greeting with a smile. The cattle buyer was a good-looking man in his early forties, dressed in black trousers, striped shirt, and black string tie.

"Are you free, Neil?" Flood inquired.

"Sure. Got those Herefords I contracted for?"

"They're out on the flats."

"Good. We can ride out right now."

Nell turned to Flood. "All right, Dave. I'm going inside and get a room. I'll see you here at six. Good-by, Mr. Gray."

Both men watched Nell stride past them to the steps. It was a stride both swift and lithe and almost masculine in quality, yet there was never a

14

woman more feminine nor more capable of arousing a man. The line of her thighs in the tight levis was sleek and clean as she moved.

As Flood moved back to his roan and Gray walked around behind him to his black gelding, three hard-bitten, range-garbed men cantered into the street. They came on toward the Tumbleweed Hotel, then at a sudden urgent gesture from the man in the lead they angled into an alley a few buildings away. Flood did not notice them, for he had turned to face Gray.

The three men remained hidden in the shadows of the alley while Flood and Gray rode past. The eyes of the watchers never left Flood. For a moment they talked animatedly together. Then one of the group issued some low-voiced instructions to his companions, received their curt nods in reply, and with battered hat pulled down low on his forehead proceeded to ride leisurely down the street in Flood's wake.

Riders kept coming and going from the depot and the loading pens and the intent, glowering rider behind Flood and Gray stirred up no interest. The man followed his quarry until they crossed the ford and swung back in the direction of the cattle he had seen hazed onto the flats just a short time before.

It did not take Gray long to complete his inspection of the Chevron herd. He rode in and out of the bunched animals, stopping now and then to lean from his saddle and examine a steer closely.

"Well, how do they look?" Flood demanded.

"I never saw finer beef cattle, Dave," Gray told him.

"What are they worth to you?"

"Fifty dollars a head. And that's the top market price."

Flood answered without hesitation. "That's a good price. They're yours, Neil."

"All right. Let's go back to the bank and settle the deal," Gray suggested. "Did you bring five hundred steers?"

"Yes. Five hundred it is. You can put your own count on them."

Gray grinned. "Hell, man, I'll take your word for it."

Back in Blue Mesa they went to the Drovers' Bank where Flood made out a bill of sale to Gray and Phillips.

"I'll give you a draft for twenty-five thousand dollars on the Kansas City National Bank," said Gray.

"No, I want it in cash," Flood told him bluntly.

Gray's sallow face registered astonishment. "But, Dave, that's too much money to carry around in a town like Blue Mesa."

Flood's ice-blue eyes flickered briefly. "Sure it is, Neil. But Tom Raines wants it that way."

"In God's name, why?"

"He lost a few thousand dollars some years ago when the bank in Capricorn went under during a drought. Ever since then he hasn't had much faith in banks."

"But twenty-five thousand dollars is another matter," persisted Gray, keeping his voice low. "Half the town must have seen you pull onto the flats with those Herefords. A lot of people have seen us together. They know I'm a buyer, that I'll be paying you for the critters."

Gray turned away as the door leading to the bank president's office opened. Gray nodded to Flood and followed him into the inner room. Simultaneously a rough-garbed man at a nearby writing table straightened up, crumpled a deposit slip in his fingers and tossed it into a wastebasket. Then he strode swiftly to the door. Outside he was joined by two other men, and all three went into the Latigo Saloon.

Meanwhile, inside the bank president's private office Flood was busy filling the pouch of a leather money belt with big-denomination bills. When the money was packed to his satisfaction, he removed his shirt, unbuttoned his undershirt, and strapped the belt around his waist.

"I still think you're making a mistake," said Gray. "Blue Mesa, like every trail town, is full of riff-raff and gun-slingers. If any of them got wind that you were carrying all that cash your life wouldn't be worth two bits."

Flood shrugged. He was aware of the risk he ran yet it did not disturb him. There was an ingrained toughness about him, a hard core that accepted each new job without any consideration of the dangers involved.

"Don't worry about me, Neil," he said. "I can take care of myself." He knotted his fist, then tapped his cedar-handled .45.

# Two

THE interior of the Latigo Saloon was dim and cool when Flood pushed through the bat-wing doors. A faint smell of sawdust and whisky and stale cigarette smoke hung in the air. The smoke lingered in a blue haze around the coal-oil lamps suspended by chains from the beamed ceiling.

Flood advanced to the bar and ordered a shot of whisky. When the drink came, he tilted the glass to his mouth and swallowed it quickly. Immediately he felt the warm bite of the liquor twisting at his belly. He ordered another drink.

The two punchers on his right finished up and tramped out of the room. Flood followed them out with his eyes, then glanced toward the far end of the bar. Three men were bunched there, drinking and talking in low voices.

Flood turned his attention back to his drink. Glass in hand, he stared over the thick rim into the flyspecked back-bar mirror. A sudden odd feeling washed over him when he saw the faces of the three men in the corner dimly reflected in the mirror. Though their features were faintly shadowed, he could see that they were watching him.

Flood's fingers tightened around the shot glass. His blue eyes narrowed. He became abruptly conscious of the pressure of the money belt strapped around his waist. With a deft motion he swallowed the whisky. The three men had left the bar now. They were strolling toward him, their spurs dragging, their long arms swinging beside their holstered six-guns.

Flood's nerves bunched in a tight knot. But not a flicker of the tension that gripped him showed in his hard-boned features. He set the glass down on the scarred pine surface of the bar and pivoted on his heel.

At that moment the leader of the group moved fully out into the light and said, "Howdy, Dave."

Flood's right hand knotted. His ice-blue eyes clung to the speaker. Instantly he recognized the man.

"It's you, Calloway," he said flatly.

The man grinned, showing crooked yellow teeth. His companions moved up on either side of him. Flood knew them too. But no smile cracked the solid gravity of his lips.

The bartender was busy serving drinks to two punchers near the door. Calloway's full lips stretched out. He said, "You don't appear glad to see us."

Flood stood straight and still before them. Quietly he answered. "I'm not."

Something dark and formless slid across Bill Calloway's square, blunt features. His thick eyebrows flattened out. The dark eyes, almost black and deeply planted in their sockets, stared hotly at Flood.

"You've got a damned short memory, my friend," he said.

"In my opinion it's too long," Flood retorted.

Ed Trotter, standing directly to Calloway's left, growled deep in his throat. He was a short, wiry man somewhere in his early forties. His thick legs were saddle-bowed and encased in threadbare levis. A limp, soggy cigarette dangled from the corner of his mouth. He was tough and irascible and some of his ingrained unpleasantness escaped in his talk. "Climb down off your high horse before you're knocked down."

Flood took one step away from the bar. Hot lights danced in his eyes. He said softly, "I'm ready any time, Ed."

Trotter's thin features twisted in a snarl. His body bent, and Flood set himself for a quick draw. But Calloway put the flat of one palm against Trotter's chest and shoved him back. "Cut it out, Ed."

"What the hell, Bill," said Nap Rickard, the third man. "Flood's got no call to act as if he was top dog in this town." Rickard was a pale-eyed, pale-skinned individual with untidy black hair. He had a narrow, sharp-angled jaw anchoring a face that was thin to the point of gauntness and ridged by a framework of jutting bones. His eyes shuttled to Flood. "You're forgetting you wouldn't be alive if it wasn't for us."

Flood's face turned grim. His words, when he spoke, were like hard chips of flint struck from a stone. "I'm not forgetting. I paid that debt with two years of my life."

Calloway's eyes brightened with mockery. He started to speak, but changed his mind. He signaled the moon-faced bartender. "A bottle of your best redeye and four glasses."

The bartender passed a bottle of whisky to him, took three silver dollars in exchange. Trotter reached for the glasses. Calloway took Flood's arm. "Come on. We'll sit down at that table near the door. I want to talk to you."

Flood resisted, his booted feet wedged solidly to the floor. "We've got nothing to talk about," he said.

Calloway grinned. It was a hard, threatening grin. The fingers of his free hand dug into Flood's arm. "That's where you're wrong, Dave."

Flood stood his ground. "Don't crowd me," he warned.

Nap Rickard slid around to Flood's left side. Suddenly he was hemmed in. Calloway was grinning, and he raised his voice jovially. "Come on. You've got time for one drink, anyway."

These three were the last men in the world Flood wished to see. He wanted no part of them.

But finally he suffered himself to be led to the table. It offered comparative privacy. He sat down in one of the crude barrel chairs facing Calloway. Trotter and Rickard seated themselves on either side of him.

Calloway twisted the cork out of the whisky bottle. He tilted the neck over Flood's glass. Flood placed his hand over the rim of the glass. "I'm not drinking," he said.

Calloway tipped the bottle over the other three glasses and poured. He looked at Flood. "What's eating you?"

"I'm remembering those two lost years." Flood's voice was tight and hard. "I've you to thank for them."

"Seems to me you're forgetting I'm the one who helped to get you out of Yuma," Calloway said.

"You picked a hell of a way to do it."

"Maybe you'd like to go back there."

Flood frowned. His voice slapped at Calloway like the sting of a whiplash. "Explain that."

Calloway waved Flood's statement aside. Deliberately he changed the subject. "That's a nice job you've got, ramrodding the Chevron outfit."

Flood sat still and straight in his chair. Nothing altered in his rough-hewn face. But his talk turned harder and flatter. "You don't miss much."

23

"My business to see things," Calloway informed him, his voice curiously bland. "You brought in some nice fat beef critters. Ought to fetch a good price."

Flood glanced at a battered clock on the saloon wall to the right of the bat-wing doors. He pushed up from his chair. "Reckon I'll move along now that we've had a talk."

Calloway's lips twisted in a slight leer. "Going to meet that pretty filly—what's her name, Nell Raines?"

Flood leaned his weight on the table top. "That's something else that doesn't concern you, Bill. So long."

"Sit down!" The command was summer-soft in tone, but there was viciousness in it and viciousness in the face Calloway lifted toward Flood. "We're not through yet."

"If you've something on your mind, let's have it." Flood eased back into his chair.

"All right. Listen to this," said Calloway. "We've got a job lined up in town and I want your help. The payoff will be worth your while."

Flood replied coldly and without hesitation. "If it's the kind of job I think it is, I'm not interested. I'm satisfied where I am."

"What do you make at the Chevron? Fifty or sixty a month? That's just drinking money for me." Calloway sneered. "The job I have in mind will pay you fifty times that."

"Once was enough. I made my mistake and the price came high."

Trotter flipped his cigarette to the floor and snapped at Calloway. "Stow it, Bill. I told you it was no use."

Calloway flicked him with a bleak glance. "Shut up. This is my party." Trotter's deep-carved, taciturn mouth curved downward and his eyes flashed angrily but he made no retort. Calloway dropped his voice another notch and went on. "We've got our eye on the Blue Mesa bank. With the trail herds coming in they've got a lot of cash on hand. I figure we can latch on to a good hunk of it. But we could use another man with a gun."

"Count me out," said Flood.

A frozen tightness ringed Calloway's long, sensuous mouth. "Think it over, Dave."

Flood's head came up. His eyes were steady and suddenly as bright as nailheads. "Get this straight, Calloway. You pushed me into one crooked deal and I got burned. That washed us up."

Both Trotter and Rickard stiffened in their seats. Trotter's teeth showed in an ugly snarl. He dropped a hand to his gun. "Damn it, Bill, you see what you've done? Now that you've spilled your guts to this jasper, what's to keep him from tipping off the sheriff?"

Calloway grinned. "Just this," he said. He dug

into a pocket of his shirt, took out a much-folded square of white glossy paper. He said, "Dave, how do you figure that Raines girl would feel if she found a reward dodger in her hotel room—a dodger with your picture on it? Or Sheriff Stack, for that matter?" Calloway's grin grew wide and wicked. "Lucky I saved this one of you." He twisted it so that Flood had a brief glimpse of his own distorted features. "It's still a pretty good likeness."

Flood looked momentarily haggard. That reward poster was the one thing that could lick him. One whisper of that and he'd be through with the Chevron—and with Nell Raines. More than that, it would put him on the run again.

But facing Calloway he steeled himself. He stood up. This time he was going—even if he had to shoot his way out.

"Well, what's the answer?" demanded Calloway.

"I'll let you know," said Flood, his mouth barely moving.

He walked to the door. Calloway and his two companions followed right behind him. Outside on the low porch Calloway said, "See me tonight. In here."

Flood paused, hating the sly smile on the dark-eyed man's face. His fist knotted. He longed to drive it against Calloway's mouth and smash all his teeth down his throat. But he throttled his anger. Turning away, he saw Nell

26

Raines standing in front of the hotel, looking in his direction. When she noticed him she waved. Flood came on toward her. Behind him Calloway's taunting call pursued him. "I'll be seeing you, Dave." After it came a laugh, hard and jeering.

# Three

NELL waited for Flood, her eyes curiously intent on the three men still bunched together in front of the saloon. She saw the big man's grin slowly fade, saw him turn to say something to his two companions, then push them on ahead of him into the saloon.

"Dave," she queried immediately as Flood reached her side, "who were those men?"

A gray veil clouded Flood's eyes. "Some punchers I used to know in Arizona."

Her thin eyebrows drew together. "They looked like hardcases to me."

"They're hard enough, I reckon," he admitted.

"Is that all?" She sensed he was holding something back. She watched his face, waiting for him to continue.

All he said was, "Let's eat. I'm hungry."

Nell colored faintly. Anger jabbed at her nerves. He had always been like that, cool and reserved and never talking about himself. He didn't want to talk about the men, and no amount of persuasion would avail.

Thinking back on his first arrival at the Chevron ranch, she realized that she actually knew little or nothing of his past. He had been a capable hand from the start, had moved into the foreman spot with a sure and solid competence.

28

But aside from saying he had worked for several years on Idaho ranches, he'd given no inkling of his past. Only now had he let slip the information that he'd known the three men in Arizona. She wondered idly if the men actually were renegades—as they looked—and why Dave should know them.

But she pushed the thought aside as Flood guided her toward a table. A waitress appeared, took their orders, and went off to the kitchen.

Nell settled back in her chair and inquired, "How did it go? With Neil Gray, I mean."

"Good. I got fifty dollars a head."

Animation caught hold of Nell's smooth features and brightened them. "That's even better than Uncle Tom expected. You have the money on you?"

"Yes."

"I don't like to see you carry it on you, Dave. Why not put it in the hotel safe overnight?"

Flood gestured with his head toward the dilapidated safe that stood on three legs near the sleepy-eyed clerk's bench. "It'll be a lot safer on me."

He met her eyes with a steady glance. Immediately she saw that it would be useless to argue the point with him.

The waitress brought their steaks, fried potatoes, and coffee. Several times during the meal Nell tried to draw Flood into further conversation without success. He had slipped into a morose and silent mood. When politeness required it, he answered her, but his replies were invariably brief and reserved. Finally, a little piqued, Nell gave up and devoted her attention to the food.

As for Flood, he welcomed the silence. It gave him time to consider the problem posed by Calloway's presence in Blue Mesa. The meeting rankled in Flood's mind. Every time he reviewed Calloway's threat of exposure he felt the wild urge to rush out of the dining room and settle the entire matter over the barrel of a smoking Colt. That was hardly the solution, however.

If he challenged Calloway, he'd have to take on Trotter and Rickard too. Though Flood was reasonably certain he could outshoot all three of them, he knew he'd never pull through if they ganged up on him. Besides, to provoke a fight in Blue Mesa involved the additional danger of exposing his own carefully concealed background.

"Shall we go, Dave?"

Nell's blunt question interrupted Flood's reflections.

"I reckon I haven't been very good company," he murmured.

She stared quizzically at him. "Something on your mind, Dave?"

"No." The answer was almost curt.

Nell flinched. She felt shut out. There *was* something on his mind, only he wasn't talking about it. Once again she found herself speculating about the three tough-grained men she'd seen with Flood. Were they responsible for his strange moodiness?

Flood rose, leaving the money for their supper on the table. Nell got up and walked out into the lobby ahead of him. She held her shoulders stiff and straight. He knew she had been offended. But at the moment there was nothing he could do about it.

Near the lobby door Nell swung around to face him. "I'm going down to Molly Ferguson to see about a dress for myself," she said, her tone cool and impersonal.

Flood smiled faintly. "Hope you find something nice."

Nell ignored his remark and said, "You won't reconsider about trying the hotel safe?"

He gestured beyond the pine board counter. "Take a look at the safe. There's your answer."

She didn't look where his hand directed. Instead, she turned and went out into the street without saying good-by.

Flood watched her go off, thinking that the night stretched out long and dismal ahead of him. The problem of what to do about Calloway gave him no peace. Going in with the man on the robbery was out of the question. But, knowing what Calloway planned, he came under an obligation. An obligation to warn the law. Calloway had an itchy trigger finger. He wouldn't stop at murder to get what he wanted.

With a weary shrug of his shoulders Flood swung in the direction of the Latigo. He strode along the walk at a rapid rate, his manner grim and preoccupied. At the Latigo he noticed that the hitch rack was filled to capacity with ponies.

Flood was halfway to the doors when Bill Calloway slid out of the shadows of an alley. Close behind Calloway walked Ed Trotter and Nap Rickard.

Calloway stopped in front of Flood, blocking his path to the saloon. "What's your answer?" he growled.

Flood glanced briefly toward the street. The sidewalk was empty of traffic in both directions. Slowly he laid his bitter, unyielding stare upon Calloway. "It's still the same," he murmured.

Passion whirled hotly through Calloway's vitals. His eyes pinched together. His mouth made a sudden cruel gash in his chunky face. He dropped his shoulders, and his hands lifted toward his gun belt.

Ed Trotter spilled out a curse and said, "Drill the damned skunk!"

Flood moved like a streak of chain lightning. Trotter was lifting out his six-shooter when Flood churned forward, bringing a right-hand punch squarely to the renegade's jaw. Trotter fell as if he had been clubbed with a fencepost. Instantly Flood whirled toward Calloway, his gun canting upward in a hard-knuckled fist.

"Go ahead, Bill," he rasped. "Burn your powder."

The big outlaw swayed on widely planted boots, his head hanging forward, his coarse features bloated with wrath. Flood's motion, swift and mercurial as a flash of light, had nailed him with his weapon only half-drawn from the holster. For one long moment his hand didn't move while he watched the long, steel barrel of Flood's gun.

Flood's face was twisted in a wicked grimace. His temper was fully aflame. It roughed him up. It tugged at his nerves, pushing him to the edge of rashness. His talk beat mercilessly at Calloway. "Come on. Let's get to it. You've been looking for a fight. It's your move!"

The challenge hit Calloway with the force of a slammed fist. Though the words were low and soft, there was no softness in their intent. And there was no break in the hard, compressed lines of Flood's face.

A long, ragged sigh dragged out of Calloway. He straightened, let his Colt slide back into its leather pouch. "You're right," he said thickly. "Mine is the next move. I'll pick my own time."

Swiftly he swung on his heel, gave Nap Rickard

a shove with his free hand, and melted into the shadows. His hard voice reached out of the darkness to pull Ed Trotter, just in the act of rising from the ground, along with him. "This way, Ed!"

Voices beat loudly from the Latigo, coming nearer. Flood sank his gun into the holster and pivoted toward the bat wings.

The bar was busy. He made a place for himself in the crowd, ordered a whisky, and drank half the glass at one gulp. Over the rim of the glass he stared at his own somber reflection in the back-bar mirror.

A clump of unruly brown hair fell down across his forehead. The skin of his face was deeply tanned by the sun and stretched taut over strong, prominent bones. His nose was straight, his jaw solid. The eyes, blue and hard, were suddenly bitter with memories.

Vividly he remembered his wild, tumultuous life after the death of his mother and father and the loss of their two-bit cattle ranch. He'd roamed through Arizona and New Mexico, taking one cowpunching job after another. He'd had a brief span with the Idaho Northern Railroad as roving trouble shooter. But when the line went bankrupt he went back to punching cows.

Then, without warning, the cattle market hit the skids. Ranchers began laying off extra hands. A long drought followed. There were no jobs. With empty pockets he followed the grub line from ranch to ranch all through southern Arizona.

At last, late one afternoon, the long drought broke and torrential rains swept the parched earth. Caught out in the open, Flood had pushed on through the storm, hoping to reach a ranch or a town before nightfall. He was soaked through and through when he came to the banks of a swollen creek.

Though he was bone-weary and his horse was jaded, Flood decided to attempt a crossing. Once he hit the water, a swift current caught him immediately. His horse lost his footing and had to swim. Flood piled out of the saddle and let himself slide backward until he had the gelding's tail, gasping for air as wave after wave broke over him.

Only half-conscious, he battled to the surface of the storm-lashed creek. Through a yellow spray of muddy water he saw the gelding far out of reach. Dimly he heard a shout from shore. He turned, water gushing over him, and saw three riders on the bank. As Flood struggled to keep his face above the savagely tossing wave crests, he saw a wide loop arch through space and land in the water inches away. He lunged forward, caught the rope in his hand. Falling face forward, he went under again. A roaring began in his ears, but he held onto the rope. Then he felt himself being hauled toward shore.

When he regained his senses he found himself in a shallow cave. A warm fire was blazing close by and three range-garbed men were hunkered around the flames watching him. Beyond them, near the entrance to the cave where the rain still pelted down, the riders' three horses as well as his own gelding were ground-tied.

That was his first meeting with Bill Calloway, Ed Trotter, and Nap Rickard. They'd spent the night in the cave, and the next day, when the creek had gone down, they crossed it and moved on into the hills.

It hadn't taken Flood long to realize that his new friends were owlhooters. Because he had nothing better to do he rode with them. And from their hard faces, their tied-down Colts, their constant wariness on the trail and their avoidance of towns—except for occasional forays for supplies—he knew these men were no grub-line riders, no cowpunchers temporarily out of work.

They hadn't talked much about themselves though they'd questioned him at some length. Then one day Calloway went off on some private and mysterious mission of his own. When he returned he informed Trotter and Rickard that everything was set. Flood's slightly puzzled frown finally prompted an explanation. Calloway told him that they planned to hold up the Prescott bank and wanted him along.

For a little while Flood had demurred. Not once

in his reckless existence had he ever stepped over the line into lawlessness. But now Calloway's invitation attracted him. It came at a time when he was down on his luck, when he didn't have a silver dollar to his name, when he couldn't land a cowpunching job for love or money. He told himself there was no way out. He had to live and he had to eat. And so he agreed to throw in his lot with the others.

They struck the bank just as it opened. There were few people abroad in Prescott at that early hour. Still, they ran into bad luck. Flood had been left with the horses while the others went inside. Calloway and Rickard were backing out of the bank with the loot when one of the tellers belatedly went for his gun. Trotter, covering Calloway's and Rickard's retreat, fired point-blank at the teller and brought him down with a shoulder wound.

That one shot aroused the town. Trotter turned and fled after Calloway and Rickard. All four men mounted quickly. But someone from a second-story window opened up on them with a Winchester. Flood's horse went down with a slug in the ribs. Calloway caught Flood and they galloped on down the street. Trotter and Rickard kept firing wildly behind them as they rode to get away. Men were running for horses, quickly forming pursuit. Finally a stray shot nailed Rickard's mount. Though the animal kept on for a mile or two, it couldn't maintain the pace necessary to outdistance the posse. And Calloway's horse, carrying double, also soon gave out.

At the end of an hour Flood and the others had been rounded up and were on their way back to Prescott and jail. A quick cow-country trial followed. All four men were sentenced to Yuma Prison. Flood drew a three-year term, the others six years each because they'd been hauled in once before on a stagecoach holdup near Tombstone.

Two bleak years followed—years Flood would never be able to forget, black and bitter days in a hot hellhole with the worst renegades that ever roamed the Southwest. He found himself forced into close association with killers, rapists, smugglers, and rustlers—the scum of the frontier. Somehow in that ugly outpost where hardened outlaws turned bestial and inhuman Flood managed to hold on to his self-respect. He kept to himself as much as possible even though it antagonized the other prisoners and particularly Calloway and his partners. He made it entirely clear to Calloway and the others that he wanted nothing further to do with them. Eventually the decision led to a brutal hand-to-hand fight with Calloway which had to be halted by guards and which sent them both to solitary for two weeks.

Flood's three-year term was almost completed when Calloway, Trotter, and Rickard pulled a prison break with some smuggled guns. Two guards were killed during the escape. Before fleeing Yuma, Calloway opened Flood's cell with stolen keys and forced him to go along. He'd tried to resist but had been beaten half-unconscious for his trouble.

Once out of Yuma with a powerful search spreading out behind them, Flood realized dismally that he was now definitely beyond the pale. This was not his idea of freedom. With two guards dead he'd be hunted like Calloway and the others. He'd be fair game for the gun of every sheriff and bounty hunter in the Southwest.

No one would believe that he had been forced along on the jailbreak. And if he were caught, the least he could expect was a rope around his neck.

The reward notices, when they appeared later, confirmed his worst fears. Like Calloway, Trotter, and Rickard he was listed as a dangerous killer. The reward was put at $500 and the notice stated that Dave Flood was wanted dead or alive!

The hunt instituted by the Yuma Prison authorities was a thorough one. After a shaky first night in which Flood and his companions were almost apprehended, they managed to steal some horses from a small ranch. Even then the pursuit persisted. Eventually they were compelled to split up in order to harass the posse.

Flood welcomed the split. He was in a killing rage at being forced into the jailbreak. The escape, added to the murder charge, would put him on the dodge for the rest of his life. He would always be looking along his back trail, looking for pursuit. Every stranger would be suspect.

And the months following the split-up proved to be just as black and uneasy as he had feared. He'd drifted north into Idaho, landed a punching job there. But he moved on when a cow-town sheriff started to show too much interest in him.

After that he never stayed long on any one ranch. He had adopted a different name and he stuck to it. But it was a hell of a life. He grew moodier and more taciturn. He avoided association with the other hands on the ranches where he worked.

It wasn't until he dropped into Wyoming and took the job with Tom Raines's Chevron outfit that he went back to using his right name. By that time a sort of savage recklessness had hold of him. He had grown tired of running, tired of constantly looking over his shoulder. Here he would stay and the devil with the consequences.

When Pete Guthrie, the Chevron foreman, went down in a stampede and was crippled, Raines offered Flood the job as ramrod. Flood took it and he'd been glad to get it. He liked working for Raines and he liked being near Raines's pretty niece, Nell—though Raines's young wife, Melody, was herself very attractive and anxious for male attention.

A tap on the shoulder drew Flood out of the dread backwash of his past. He turned, half-expecting to see Calloway again. But it was Neil Gray, the cattle buyer.

"Feel like some poker, Dave?" Gray asked. "Couple of cowmen I know are hankering to play. Thought you might want to join us."

Flood grinned, a rare thing for him. "Neil, you've asked me at just the right time. I'll be glad to play."

At first Flood gave the cards his full attention, but after a time his mind began to wander. When midnight came he dropped out and went back to the hotel.

The clerk was asleep in his chair behind the counter when Flood strode by and mounted the stairs. The lobby was deserted and the dining room was a dark nave of ghostly tables and shadowy, empty chairs.

Upstairs on the second floor of the hotel the corridor was dark. The lamp that usually hung from the ceiling had gone out. Flood had to grope his way along the hall to his own door. Key in hand, he felt for the lock with his finger. Finding the opening, he thrust in the key, turned it, and pushed the door open.

Inside the room was completely black except for a gray square of light where the single, thinly curtained window faced the rear alley.

Abruptly two things happened. The door, which

41

he had left slightly ajar, slammed shut. As he whirled in that direction the hard round core of a gun barrel was jammed into his ribs.

"Hold it, Dave!" came the crisp command in the darkness. "Don't move if you want to go on living." The voice was Calloway's.

A freezing tightness closed down on Flood's mind. "What do you want?" he demanded. Every nerve was bunched up, ready to uncoil with the lash of action. Only the bite of hard steel in his flesh held him back.

"Your gun first, Dave," whispered Calloway. "The rest you can guess." His tone sharpened. "All right, Ed. Take him!"

# Four

CALLOWAY'S sharp command to Ed Trotter spun Flood into action. Trotter's rush carried its warning note in the noisy slap of boots moving across the board floor. Flood whirled away from the unseen attack, going for his gun. Then a heavy body crashed into him. A hand ripped at his holster. Flood struck blindly at his assailant in the dark, feeling his knuckles rake the side of someone's head. Simultaneously he was hit from behind. Dimly he felt someone fumbling at his shirt, ripping fiercely at the money belt strapped around his waist. Then he lost track of everything for a little while.

The door of his room burst inward and a small knot of men appeared in the hall. They were led by the sleepy-eyed clerk, now painfully alert, with a lantern gripped in his bony fist.

Propped on one knee, Flood glanced grimly toward the curious group.

"You're a little late," he murmured.

"What's happened?" demanded the hotel clerk.

The men came on into the room. A lanky red-haired puncher glanced at Flood's torn, gaping shirt. "Looks like you've been robbed. Were you carrying a money belt?"

"Yeah," replied Flood curtly. He got to his feet and limped across the room to the window. Then he called over his shoulder. "Bring the lantern here a moment."

The clerk shuffled over to join him. Flood stared into the alley. Below the window there was a short drop to a low shed roof. And from the shed it was just another few feet to the ground. This, then, was Calloway's avenue of entrance and escape. It was easy enough, once the number of his room was known.

"You lose much, friend?" demanded the red-haired cowboy.

Flood ignored the man and caught the hotel clerk in a hard grip. "My name's Flood," he grated. "Did you give the number of my room to anybody tonight?"

"No—no. Of course not," the clerk stammered.

Flood brought his face close to the clerk's. Flood's eyes were red-flecked and challenging. "I want the truth," he said.

"That's the truth," the clerk replied. "I swear it is. Things were slow tonight. The only business I had at all was when three cowhands came in looking for rooms."

"Three men?" demanded Flood.

"Yeah. But we're full up. I couldn't give them anything."

"And I suppose the register is always out on the counter where anyone can look at it."

The clerk reddened. "You—you don't mean those men—?"

44

Flood cut him short. "I mean just that."

He tucked his shirt into the waistband of his trousers, then moved to the side wall to retrieve his gun. Shoving it back into his holster, he strode out into the hall.

"If you're going after those fellows," said the redhead, "you'd better rouse the sheriff."

Flood walked on, unheeding. Behind him trooped the others. A door was flung open, and Nell Raines, a quilted robe draped about her willowy figure, stepped out. She took one look at his bruised face and the ragged gap in his flannel shirt and cried: "What is it, Dave? The money— did you—?"

"It's gone," Flood said curtly, not letting her finish.

He strode past her and started down the stairs.

"Wait, Dave!" she said.

"Later—not now," he said, and continued down to the lobby with the crowd at his heels.

Cutting toward the rear of the lobby, he pushed through a small back door that led to a littered alley. Reaching the sloping shed below his room, Flood hunkered down to examine the earth for hoofprints.

The hotel clerk came forward with the lantern. By its glow Flood saw the distinct mark of shod hoofs. Three horses had stood tethered to a scrawny cottonwood tree that leaned toward the shed. The prints were superimposed, one over the

45

other, but out of the welter of sign he noted the trail spearing away through the alley.

If Calloway and his friends had gone eastward toward the mesa and the high ridges beyond it there might be a chance of picking up a clear trail since there wasn't too much traffic in that direction.

But a brief inspection showed Flood that he was doomed to disappointment. The trail of the three riders, after cutting along the edges of the alley that ran behind the town's main stores, finally wound back to the dusty wagon road.

Still on foot and with the lantern bobbing in his hand, casting odd, elongated shadows up and down the street and across the slatted board fronts of the buildings, Flood drew to a halt. With the constant heavy travel on the road it would be impossible to pick out any distinct sign. The butter-yellow light issuing from the lantern illumined a broad strip of ground, literally honeycombed with the prints of horses' hoofs and the wheel marks of rumbling freight wagons.

Calloway had chosen his escape route carefully. The road crossed Little Teton Creek at the ford, then debouched on the prairie—a prairie which in recent weeks had seen the passage of thousands of cattle moving down from all of northern and western Wyoming to the railroad loading pens. No man—no matter how clever a reader of trail sign—would be able to ferret out Calloway's line of retreat.

"It's no use," Flood said wearily. "We'll never pick up their trail in this mess of prints."

He walked on ahead of the crowd, his boots gouging out great chunks of dry earth. His stride was a measure of the rage that was consuming him. He had been responsible for the Chevron trail herd money, yet he had let it be taken away from him.

Although he knew who his assailants were, they had gotten clean away. With the money they'd taken from him they wouldn't have to worry about hitting the Blue Mesa Bank. Twenty-five thousand dollars would keep them in whisky and women for a long time to come.

Anger rolled around in Flood's vitals. It was like a great pulse, beating in his brain and in every nerve fiber of his body. He came to the hotel and swung sharply in from the walk.

Nell was waiting for him in the lobby. She had dressed in an old pair of blue jeans and a wrinkled man's shirt open low at the throat. She had been walking up and down the lobby in a sort of restrained fury.

"I don't suppose you had any luck," she said.

"No," Flood replied, his features tight and cold.

"Come on upstairs," Nell said. "I want to talk to you."

There was an icy chill in Nell's eyes Flood

didn't like. She turned from him with a fluid swing of lithe hips and mounted the stairs ahead of him. He followed.

The door of Nell's room was open. A lamp guttered on the table near the iron bed. Nell walked right in. Flood stopped halfway across the room as she moved to the table and whirled on him.

"Close the door," she ordered.

Again Flood looked at her. "Do you realize it's after midnight?"

Scorn bit into Nell's mouth, drawing it tight. "If you're thinking about my reputation, you can forget it," she said. "I don't want everyone in the hotel to hear what we have to say."

"Suit yourself," Flood said.

He walked back to the door and pushed it shut. Then he turned and faced her across half the width of the small bare room. He was shocked by the antagonism he saw in her eyes. She was like an utter stranger, all the light gone out of her face. In its place was a dark, rigid intentness.

"Tell me what happened," she directed.

Briefly he repeated the sequence of events that had occurred after he had walked into his hotel room.

Nell listened stonily. When Flood had finished she said with a thin twist of her lips, "That fixes the Chevron. I guess you understand that."

"Sorry, Nell. I did my damnedest—but it wasn't enough."

48

"Being sorry doesn't help," she snapped. "Uncle Tom was a fool to insist on your taking payment from Neil Gray in cash. And you should have put the money in the hotel safe."

"You're right about that, I reckon," Flood admitted.

Nell strode to the window, stared blindly at the drawn shade, then came back to a spot within a few feet of him. He had never seen her so upset and angry. He watched the aroused breathing that lifted her full bosom so clearly outlined beneath the low-cut man's shirt.

"Have you any ideas about where Uncle Tom will get the money to climb out of debt?" she inquired with caustic irony.

Flood's face was gray and hard as a piece of flint. A severe light lay in his blue eyes. "I know only one thing at this moment," he said.

"What's that?" Nell demanded.

"I won't rest until I get that money back."

"Maybe you know where to look for it," she suggested.

"I've got an idea," he told her flatly.

Nell's lips thinned. "Where would that be?"

"The Teton Mountains," Flood replied. "It's the best place for a man on the run to hide out."

"Maybe you know more than that." The dark stain of suspicion colored her words.

Flood lifted his head in surprise. She was so near to him, yet it seemed to him that an

49

impenetrable wall had risen between them.

"If you mean that I know the men I want, you're right," Flood said after a long moment of silence.

Nell's features did not relent. "It's time for you to talk," she said.

"About what?" Flood countered.

"About those three men I saw you with this afternoon, for one thing." Her red mouth was ridged and firm. "Those men were renegades. I could tell just by looking at them. Yet you seemed to be on friendly terms with them."

A barely perceptible flush seeped through the bronze hue of Flood's weather-burned skin. "They're no friends of mine."

"Who are they, then?"

"Their names wouldn't mean anything to you."

Nell's reply was sharp, like the deft stroke of a rapier in a fencer's hand. "They might mean something to Sheriff Syd Stack."

Flood shrugged. "I wouldn't know about that." He kept his eyes level and direct. But he wasn't good at dissembling and he wondered if Nell really believed him. Hurriedly he switched his attention to the heart of their discussion. "As far as the money goes, I'm not giving up on it. I'll hit the trail for the Tetons first thing in the morning."

Nell's voice came back at him with sharp, whetted scorn. "And when you go, that'll be the last the Chevron will see of you."

He saw the hard blue shine of her eyes, shutting him away from her. Suddenly he could no longer tolerate the barrier that had come between them. He grabbed her and pulled her roughly into his arms. "I don't like your talk," he said.

Nell did not draw back. Her supple, well-formed body lay passively within the tight circle of his right arm. She gazed directly at him. "Let me go," she said. It was not an appeal but a curt command.

"Not until I've finished," he told her. Faintly he caught the rhythm of Nell's heart beating against his chest. And the warm curve of her mouth so close to his own almost drove him mad.

"Go on," she said, still not fighting him, still coldly unresponsive.

Flood frowned intently. "I'm still the same man—the man you seemed to enjoy kissing one afternoon a few weeks ago."

Nell's eyes narrowed. "That was a mistake. It won't happen again."

The roaring inside Flood was more compelling now. It unsettled him. "Don't count on that," he murmured thickly. "What happened tonight hasn't changed anything for me." Deliberately he bent his head and kissed her.

The touch of Flood's lips was a current ticking off a swift explosion in the girl. She thrust the palms of her hands against Flood's chest, pushed savagely away from him. At the same instant that she broke out of the embrace her swinging right hand slapped his cheek.

"It has for me, Dave," she declared. "I'm thinking that neither Uncle Tom Raines nor anyone else on the Chevron knows much about you—where you come from or what you did before you turned up at the Chevron hunting a job."

The sting of the blow left a burning sensation on Flood's cheek. He could feel the imprint of each of Nell's fingers on his flesh. She had hit hard. And her talk now was just as hard. Slowly his pride began to take over and with it came a rage that matched her own.

"Rather late to be thinking of my past, isn't it?" he asked.

"Perhaps. But you can remedy that by doing some talking."

Resolution darkened Flood's face. "This isn't the time for it," he said flatly, and swung toward the door.

# Five

FLOOD had breakfast the next morning in a small restaurant across the street from the livery barn where he had stabled the gelding. He had no desire to meet Nell in the hotel dining room after their hostile parting. Besides, the time for talking had passed. He had to move and move fast if he hoped to catch up with Calloway.

Nell's readiness to suspect him of complicity in the theft of the Chevron cash left him with an acid taste in his mouth. Always mercurial in temper and quick to take offense, Nell had gone off the deep end in veering so sharply against him. It left him bewildered and angry.

One thing was certain, however. He had presumed too much from the one chance meeting when she had permitted him to kiss her. She had closed the door between them with a finality that was shocking.

After hurrying through a meager meal of bacon and eggs, dry bread and coffee, he crossed to the livery and got his roan gelding. He had paid the hostler and had saddled up before he noted that the gelding's right forehoof needed reshoeing.

Because he realized he had days of tough riding ahead of him he decided that, no matter how much it delayed him, the hoof had to be reshoed. Accordingly, he took the gelding over to the blacksmith where he had to wait for the smith to finish shoeing a big Morgan horse before the roan could be taken care of.

At last he rode out of the blacksmith's compound and cantered down the street toward Little Teton Creek.

Only a few people were abroad at the early hour. A ranch buckboard was drawn up before the loading platform of the Mercantile. Two saddle horses were tethered to the rail in front of the Shorthorn Saloon. And farther down the street a freight wagon was lumbering toward the railroad.

Then as Flood drew near the bank he spotted something that tightened every nerve in his body. Three saddled horses stood half in the shadows of the alley between the bank and an empty feed store. He looked sharply toward the saddlers, then stiffened when he saw a man's crouched shape half-hidden by the farthest horse.

The watcher's head popped into view. Flood went hot all over. The man was Nap Rickard!

Suddenly Flood knew that he had completely underestimated Calloway. He piled out of the saddle, rushed under the bank's hitch rack as Rickard darted forward to intercept him.

At the same moment a man's hoarse, angry yell drifted from the interior of the bank. The yell was followed by a shot. Through the half-open door, their backs to him, came Calloway and Trotter.

Trotter held a cloth bag filled with coin and currency. He had a gun in his hand.

Calloway had two weapons. From the barrel of one gun a thin streamer of smoke still dribbled.

Trotter saw Flood at the very instant Flood's warning slicked through the morning stillness.

"Hold it!"

"Let's fan it, Bill!" Trotter shouted to Calloway.

The skinny outlaw swiveled his gun around and fired at Flood. The bullet drilled an inch past Flood's face. He brought his own weapon into play, aiming for Trotter's legs. But the shot went wild. He was dimly aware that Rickard had also fired at him and missed. Then Calloway hurtled savagely against him. Calloway's hand moved up and down in a rapid arc. The barrel of the outlaw's gun descended toward Flood's head. Flood wrenched to one side, took the blow on the shoulder. The crunching impact drew a gasp of pain from Flood. His right arm from shoulder to fingers went numb. His Colt spilled from his fingers.

He dropped to the ground, scrambling for the weapon. But he forgot his quest as the street came alive to the beat of men's yells. Suddenly the town, empty just scant seconds before, boiled with furious activity. The doors of the Shorthorn Saloon flew open. Two men spilled out, guns in hand. One man yelled: "Holdup. At the bank!"

A stray shot pounded through the air, singing

55

past Calloway. Then came a brace of shots as the man's partner began triggering his Colt. Both men came at a lumbering run down the street. Across the way from the saloon a third man bounded from a store. A fourth darted out of the livery barn in the opposite direction. And from the sheriff's office beyond the next intersection appeared the dark, stocky shape of Sheriff Stack and one of his deputies.

"Nap! Bring the horses up!" yelled Calloway.

Rickard spun around and dashed back for their mounts. He grabbed the reins and lumbered over to Calloway and Trotter. A man appeared in the bank doorway. There was a Colt in his hand. He drew a slow bead on Trotter. But a snap shot from Calloway drove the fellow back inside.

Then Rickard was up with the horses. All three men swung into their saddles. Flood groped painfully to his feet. There was a dull ache along the top of his shoulder. A fierce, needle-hot tingling ran down the nerves of his arm. He made a lunge for his own roan gelding at the edge of the hitching rail. But Rickard's piebald horse, turned spooky by the gunfire, crashed into the roan with a high-pitched whinny. The roan squealed as the piebald's forehoofs ripped a sliver of flesh from its withers. Before Flood could reach the roan the animal had bolted off down the street, closely followed by Rickard.

A short distance behind Rickard came Ed

Trotter. He turned in the saddle and emptied his gun at the straggling line of men racing to stop their escape. Calloway, the last to mount, also fired in the direction of the townsmen. He dropped one man with a bullet in the thigh, then spurred after his companions.

Flood darted under the hitch rack, sprinted through the dust of the road, and flung himself at Calloway as the outlaw urged his mount into a gallop. Somehow Flood's high leap carried him half into Calloway's saddle. Calloway struck at him with the barrel of his gun. The sharp metal edge of the sight grazed Flood's left cheek. Instantly a thin streak of scarlet threaded Flood's tanned flesh. But he hung on, one hand gripping the near horn of Calloway's saddle.

The outlaw's horse continued its wild gallop down the street. And behind them guns rattled ominously as more men threw themselves into the fray, hoping to cut off Calloway from his companions.

Flood tried to haul himself all the way into the saddle, at the same time striking at Calloway with his left hand. But the effort was too much. There wasn't much strength in his right arm. And he couldn't fight off the savage, down-chopping arc of Calloway's gun hand. He took a hard rap on his left forearm. Then another blow broke through his guard and rammed the side of his head. The fingers of his right hand lost their purchase on

Calloway's saddle horn and he slid to the ground.

Dimly Flood heard the beat of hoofs going away from him as Calloway lashed his horse into a dead run. Sporadic six-gun fire sieved the air above Flood's head. Slowly he dragged himself to his knees. There was a dull ringing in his head. His vision wasn't entirely clear. But he knew he couldn't black out now. He bit his tongue until he felt the salty taste of blood in his mouth. The pain sent the tide of blackness ebbing away.

When he got to his feet he stumbled right into the arms of two men. It came as a distinct shock to hear the man on his right shout to the crowd behind them:

"Here's one of the buskies!"

Another voice answered stridently from the rear. "Hold on to him! Don't let him get away."

As Flood's eyes cleared he saw the hot glare of rage in the faces of his captors. He struggled to get free. But in his weakened state his efforts proved futile. The grip on his arms only grew tighter.

Then Sheriff Stack and a small group of men—all of them panting from their mad dash down the street—came up. The lawman was thickset, yet quite tall and lithe-limbed. His cheeks were lined and hollow under a sharp ledge of bone. A thick, untrimmed mustache covered his long upper lip. There was a seedy, unkempt look about him.

Now he whirled around to survey the crowd. "I

want a posse. Quick. Everybody with a horse, mount up and be ready to ride before those jaspers get clear away!"

A good portion of the crowd melted away. Most of the men headed for the livery barn. The sheriff yelled after them. "Someone bring up a horse for me. Make it pronto!"

Stack turned back to Flood. "No use struggling, friend. Looks like you were caught dead to rights."

A puncher hurried out of the bank. His excited yell carried to the small group lingering around Flood and the sheriff. "Hey, Sheriff! The bandits got Harvey Long, one of the bank tellers. He's hurt pretty bad, I reckon."

"All right!" snapped Stack. "Don't waste time telling me. Go and get the doc!" The lawman fastened his glowering attention upon Flood. "As for you, my friend, you'd better start praying that Long pulls through or you'll be facing a murder charge!"

Flood tried to wrench away from the men holding him prisoner. "This is crazy, Sheriff," he said. "I'm Dave Flood of the Chevron outfit. I was trying to stop that one outlaw from getting away. I barged into them just as they were coming out of the bank."

"That's not the way it looked to me!" growled the sheriff. "I saw you with those other jaspers making for your horse. One of the critters bucked into your saddler and sent him busting down the street. You tried to grab a ride with one of your pards and got tossed off for your trouble."

"Yeah, that's the way of it," added a lean, gaunt-looking puncher. "When things go wrong with polecats like this jasper, it's everybody for himself." The puncher bent his hostile gaze on Flood. "Your friend sure wasn't hankering to ride double. He was just thinking of his own skin."

"Stack!" rasped Flood, anger stirring in him. "You've got to listen to me. I don't care how this thing looks. I tried to stop them—"

"Tell me later," snapped Stack as a bunch of townsmen came back from the livery and one of the men led a horse up to him. The lawman turned to a lean, hawk-nosed man with sallow wrinkled skin and a battered deputy's star pinned to his shirt. "Throw this bucko in the calaboose till I get back with the posse!" He lifted his voice. "All right. Hit your saddles!"

With a loud clash of riding gear and an occasional exuberant shout the posse hammered out of Blue Mesa. Their going left Flood with a lost, barren feeling. He jerked his head at the deputy. But before he could say a word the deputy growled a command to the two men still holding Flood.

"Come on. Let's get this fellow into jail."

Fighting them every step of the way, Flood was

literally dragged down the street to the jail. There a puncher appeared with the roan.

"I reckon here's this fellow's horse," he said.

"Yeah," said Flood, "and take a good look at the brand he's wearing! It's the Chevron brand and I'm Dave Flood, ramrod for the Chevron outfit."

"Maybe so," grunted the deputy. "That still doesn't clear you of that bank job."

More people were gathering around the jail entrance now. The puncher who had found the roan led the horse to the head of the alley and left him there. Flood glanced at the roan, then at the newcomers. Forcing her way through the small crowd came Nell Raines.

"Nell!" he called. "Tell this damned deputy who I am."

The girl came forward. Men broke ground to make a path for her. She looked hard at Flood, not smiling and not giving him any sign of recognition, then turned to the deputy.

"I've heard about the attempt to rob the bank," she said.

"It was more than an attempt, ma'am," said the deputy. "The jaspers got away with quite a haul—all except this man. Do you know him?"

"Yes, I know him," she said.

Grimness touched Flood's battered face. There was no friendliness for him in Nell's eyes. He saw that she was ready to believe anything she was told by the crowd.

"How well do you know him?" the deputy demanded.

"He's Dave Flood, foreman of the Chevron ranch at the northern edge of the Tetons. I'm Nell Raines, niece of Tom Raines, the Chevron owner."

The deputy considered that information with a gray doubt slowly forming in his mind. "Hell, maybe Flood's story is right."

"What's his story?" Nell asked.

The deputy repeated the sheriff's version of what had occurred from the moment the outlaws made a run for their horses, then added Flood's account of his own part in that action.

Nell's eyes gleamed with sharp malice. "How many men did you say took part in the raid?"

"Four—counting Flood."

"I'm not surprised," she said.

Flood shot an appeal to Nell. "Be sure you know what you're doing, Nell."

"I know well enough," she retorted.

"Get on with it, ma'am," directed the deputy. "We can't stand in the middle of the street all day."

"It's just this," she said slowly, choosing her words with care. "The Chevron's been careless in hiring its help. We came in with a herd of Herefords yesterday. Last night Flood was attacked and robbed in his room. He was carrying the trail herd money on him. Before that—in the afternoon—I saw him with three men. They were a hard-looking lot. Flood obviously was acquainted with them. Yet, when I questioned him, he refused to talk about them. Now you tell me about this bank robbery. Again there are three men—and Flood. Add it up. What do you get for an answer?"

Nell's indictment of Flood was greeted by an ominous, strained stillness. Flood took one look at the small crowd of men surrounding him and saw that Nell had convicted him in their eyes.

"Hell," said one of the onlookers, a portly store owner, "this man is obviously one of the renegades. Throw him in jail and have done with it."

"It'll be more than a cell in the calaboose for him if that bank teller dies," growled a swarthy cowpuncher.

"A rope around his neck is what he needs!" said another.

The deputy, suddenly nervous at the turning tide in the crowd's emotions, held up his hand. "Enough of that kind of talk. This gent waits in jail until the sheriff gets back. I don't want any trouble with any of you." His fingers tightened around his Colt, but his mouth went a little slack with queasy fear.

The swarthy puncher laughed unpleasantly. "Won't be any trouble at all taking him off your hands."

A queer, straining intensity rolled through Flood. With a vicious wrench of his muscular body he ripped free of his two captors and charged the deputy. The lawman made a belated attempt to swivel his gun around. Flood knocked it aside, then sent the deputy reeling with a roundhouse swing to the point of his chin. The deputy whirled off balance and crashed into two cowpunchers. All three men went down in an ungainly heap.

Flood leaped over them and grabbed Nell around the waist. A swoop of his right hand lifted her .38 revolver out of the holster snugged against her hip. She struggled fiercely to get free. But he whipped her body up against him and retreated past the mouth of the alley, heading toward the door of the empty feed barn.

"Hold it, everybody!" he warned in a voice that was utterly cool and deadly. "At this range a thirty-eight can drill a big hole in a man's chest."

The deputy got to his feet, cursing. "Hiding behind a woman!" he growled. He groped for his gun.

Flood's command halted the deputy. "Leave it lay. The rest of you stay clear." He broke off as Nell struggled savagely to free herself. She clubbed at his arms, tried to scratch his face with her nails. Flood spoke to her grimly. "Sorry I've got to do this, Nell. You forced my hand."

She cried out angrily, "You'll never get away."

"The girl's right," snapped the deputy as he began to edge forward, the crowd at his back. Some of the men still held their guns but they couldn't get a clear shot at Flood as he retreated toward the feed barn.

"I figure I can make it," said Flood grimly. "But I'll be back. And if my luck holds I'll bring every cent of that stolen bank money. You can leave that message with the sheriff. You gents have me pegged as an outlaw. It's a cinch I won't get a chance to change your minds if I sit in a jail cell."

Flood felt the warped door of the feed barn behind him. He slammed the weight of his shoulders against the panels. The door burst inward. He almost fell with Nell on top of him. But he caught his balance, pushed Nell to one side, and said, "So long, Nell."

Then he slammed the door shut behind him. The barn was musty and gloomy. Some dry bales of hay lay around. There were also a number of cases stacked near the door. There was a door in the far wall that obviously gave out on the alley.

All this Flood saw in a split-second glance. A yell from outside told him the crowd was ready to assault the door. He pushed a couple of cases against the door. He heard the deputy yell, "Get around the back, some of you gents, and cut him off!"

There was a concerted rush down the alley as the crowd divided and men lumbered around to the alley. At the same time the front door shivered under the impact of a wild rush. It slid partly open as two of the impeding cases were shoved back a notch.

"Keep low!" someone yelled. "The jasper's got a gun."

Flood crouched in the shadows behind a high case set against the wall and close to the door. He was relying on an old trick to get free. If the men out front behaved as he expected, they would trample down the front door and go charging through the barn, hoping to push him into the arms of their fellows in the alley.

There was another assault upon the door. This time it swept the bunched wooden cases to one side. Five men, crouched low with guns in their fists, hurtled through the opening.

"Spread out and keep your eyes peeled!" one of them cried.

They moved on with a rush into the murky half-light of the barn. Flood waited just a few seconds until they had cleared the door. Then he slid from his place of concealment and raced out to the street. A running man, late in joining the activities, sprinted across the dust. He slid to a halt, groping for his gun.

Flood charged him and knocked him flat with a well-timed blow of the .38 barrel. A cry halfway behind him jerked him around. It was Nell. He turned, raced toward the roan still standing at the head of the alley. Nell tried to intercept him.

He reached the gelding, flipped up the reins, and vaulted into the saddle. Nell threw herself at the animal, one arm lifted to grab the reins. Flood pivoted the gelding out of reach. His eyes were bitter as they met hers. "I'll remember this, Nell," he said.

Then he swung away, straight down the street, as a couple of men, alerted by Nell's first cry of warning, appeared from the feed barn and flung a few wild shots in his direction.

The bullets fell harmlessly to the dust as Flood galloped out of six-gun range, racing toward Little Teton Creek.

# Six

NELL watched the forming of another posse with a dark, brooding attention. Flood had gotten clear of Blue Mesa without a bullet touching him. Precious minutes sped by while the deputy and the other men who had broken into the feed barn rounded up horses for the pursuit. After they had gone boiling out of town in a great cloud of gray alkali she wandered back to the hotel.

The white-hot flame of rage still burned inside Nell. Though she had acted purely on impulse from the moment she noticed Flood in the hands of the crowd, she still felt that she had been justified. Everything pointed to Flood's implication in the bank robbery. And she was now quite certain that the attack on Flood in the hotel room had been arranged by him and the three hardcases she had seen with him the afternoon before.

Somehow Flood's defection left her personally outraged. She admitted to herself with a slow reluctance that she had begun to care for the Chevron ramrod. She admired his sinewy strength, his competence in taking over the details of running the ranch. And if he was often silent and reserved, that, too, had been an attraction.

Other men had courted her. But Flood with his

taciturn hardness, his unbreakable reserve, and the complete lack of interest he had shown toward her during his early months at the Chevron had intrigued her as no other man had ever done.

The afternoon she had let him kiss her was as deeply engraved on her memory as it was on Flood's though she would have died rather than let him know it. She hadn't even been thinking of him when they met up in the hills. And what had happened after they'd ridden together and talked for more than a half hour had come with the suddenness of an electric shock.

She remembered with a sense of shame how she had poured all of herself out to him through her eager lips. She had wanted him to kiss her. The sensation had been entirely new and wonderful to her and also a little frightening.

Now as she walked into the lobby of the hotel she scrubbed at her lips with her fingers. The weight of his own mouth seemed to linger there. It was a pressure she could not erase. And it angered her, for she had allowed herself to be betrayed. She felt unclean.

But one thing saddened her. That was Flood's taking refuge behind her to make his escape. It was completely out of character. It was the action of a man who was either a coward or driven to the point of desperation by circumstances beyond his control. She hated him for that. She had wanted to see him caught by the crowd. Yet the moment he turned away from her on the gelding and his dark and bitter gaze fastened on her she found herself assailed by conflicting emotions—emotions she couldn't quite fathom.

Those same feelings hit Nell now, trailing a gray thread of worry through her mind. But she thrust them aside, hugging the familiar sense of outrage to herself.

She checked out of the hotel and went immediately to the livery barn for her horse. After the attendant had saddled the mare for her, she climbed into the saddle and rode out toward the flats where Hoot Ellison waited with the Chevron beef herd.

She rode up to the Chevron camp in a flurry of dust, jumped to the ground, and walked straight to Ellison, who was hunkered by the remains of a fire, fashioning a cigarette with nimble fingers. The tight, dark color of her normally light eyes sent Ellison surging to his feet.

"What's wrong, Nell?" he asked. "Did something happen to Flood?"

"Plenty," snapped Nell. "And none of it is good. The trail herd cash is gone and Dave is running for the hills with a posse on his heels."

Ellison moved nearer.

"But why should a posse be chasing Dave?" Ellison demanded. "It doesn't make sense."

"It will when you hear what happened," Nell

70

told him. Then in words that still shook with the tumult of her anger she gave Ellison an account of the events that had occurred since she and Flood had ridden away from camp the previous afternoon. "Dave is a renegade and a thief," she concluded hotly. "He's made a fool of all of us."

Ellison's thin, ruddy face stiffened in surprise. "Nell, I can't believe it."

"Every word of it is true," she snapped. "I saw Dave with those three gun-slicks yesterday afternoon. Then came the robbery—if you can call it that—in the hotel. And this morning the bank was held up—by four men. Among them was Dave. It all ties in."

Ellison scrubbed a calloused palm across his beard-stubbled cheeks. "I would have taken my oath that Dave was a straight shooter," he stated. "Not that any of us knows much about him or where he came from. But he was a damned good man with a rope. He knows cattle, and I never saw a fellow work harder."

"Well, he's gone now," said Nell. "And with him went every cent of the trail herd money that the Chevron needed to get out of debt." The acid stab of vexation twisted her insides. "There's nothing for us to do here now, Hoot. You can leave Whip Anders and Chuck Ryerson with the beef. Neil Gray will contact them later about moving the critters down to the loading pens as soon as he's arranged for some railroad cars.

71

Meanwhile, we'd better strike out for home. My uncle must be told the news without further delay."

Within an hour all arrangements had been made for delivery of the Chevron Herefords to the loading pens in town. Whip Anders and Chuck Ryerson had been instructed to see that every head was hazed into Neil Gray's cars before returning to the home ranch.

The Chevron outfit was situated in a green fold of the Teton foothills ten miles from the cow town of Capricorn. It had good graze on the lower meadows close to the ranch. And up along the higher ridges there was many a grassy bench where the Chevron Herefords could find fattening fodder.

The ranch itself was a sprawling one-story affair built some fifteen years before. The once-white clapboards were now weathered and gray, though here and there flecks of white paint still clung to the wood. There was a small truck garden behind the house. Farther away, perched along a short slope, were the log bunkhouse, a horse corral, a barn, a breaking pen for wild broncs, and a larger corral for holding cattle.

A hefty, broad-shouldered man was inside the horse corral circling warily around the skittish broncs, his sun-squinted eyes searching for a rangy dun gelding.

Suddenly the man spotted the dun. The loosely held lass rope in his hand snaked out to settle neatly around the animal's neck. He drew the noose taut, then hauled the dun out of the corral. He reached up to the top pole of the fence for his saddle and blanket and cinched the high-horned saddle into place. He was a good three inches over six feet and, though firm muscles still spanned his chest, he was beginning to show his forty-two years in the slight paunchiness around his belt.

He lifted his weight into the worn hull and cantered toward the ranch house. As he stopped near the kitchen door a tall, beautiful girl, her jet-black hair shining in the sun, came around the side of the house.

Tom Raines swung down from the saddle. He gave his young wife a broad smile. "I was fixing to stop by before I rode off," he said.

Melody Raines halted. At thirty there was a lush maturity to her high-breasted body. She was wearing a man's yellow chambray shirt. It fitted snugly, boldly outlining the swell of her bosom. The brown divided riding skirt flared out from her hips and clung lovingly, almost sensuously to her thighs. She had a clear-skinned oval face and there was a sultry warmth in the jade-green eyes she turned on Raines.

"I suppose you're off to the hills again," she said.

"Yeah. Want to take a look at things up at the Wind River line camp. I may want to move some yearlings up there next month." Raines's thin eyebrows quirked as he bent toward her. "You don't look pleased."

"Why should I be?" she said. "It's the same routine day in and day out. You're up at dawn and out in the hills till sundown or dark. We don't go anywhere and we don't see anyone."

There was a sullen, challenging expression on her features. Raines, a dour man and pretty much set in his ways, said bluntly: "I told you what it would be like on the Chevron."

His eyes flashed. "I've given you everything you've ever asked for."

"Everything except a good time," she said with an angry toss of her black-haired head.

She was in a black and bitter mood. It was an end result of her aching realization that she had made a mistake in marrying Tom Raines.

Though he didn't know it, he had caught Melody on the rebound from a violent but unhappy affair with a Kansas City railroad tycoon. All her life she had had her eye on the main chance. She'd had affairs with younger men, but she had not been long in learning that the younger men seldom owned the kind of money she was interested in.

The affair with the Kansas City railroad man might have ended up in marriage if he hadn't discovered that she was still seeing other men. The break had been sudden. And when Melody met Tom Raines while he was on a trip East seeing cattle buyers she made a quick decision.

Raines, though considerably older than herself, had the rough-and-ready hardiness of the western ranchman. And he had money. The idea of being the wife of one of Wyoming's most influential cowmen became more and more appealing.

It hadn't required much of an effort on Melody's part to get Raines to ask her to marry him. He had never had much time for women in the wild rush of hewing the Chevron ranch out of the wilderness. The lonely life on a ranch had become like second nature to him. Yet the fires of passion lay deep within him, and Melody had turned those fires loose.

They were married after an acquaintance of five days. And when they arrived in Capricorn the entire range was treated to a surprise. No one expected that Raines would ever take a wife. And more than one sun-browned, leathery-skinned cowpuncher and ranch owner found himself envying big Tom Raines for the lush, beautiful woman who shared his bed.

There had been a gigantic barbecue at the Chevron ranch. Melody had liked being the center of attraction and if the other ranch women were not overly friendly she didn't notice it.

Once the barbecue was over the Chevron outfit

settled down to routine. There were no visits to other outfits. Melody found herself isolated on the ranch with only Nell, her husband's niece, for company. And from the moment of their first meeting antagonism and dislike had sprung up between the two women. It was due, for the most part, to Nell's intuitive knowledge that for Melody her marriage to big Tom Raines had been one of pure convenience.

As if from a great distance Melody heard Raines's clipped voice speaking to her. "There's more to living than just having a good time."

"You'll never prove that to me," she said curtly.

Temper rolled a bright red streak of blood into Raines's weather-seamed features. A quick retort came to his lips, but he stilled it. The pull of her nearness did that to him.

"Why not take a ride?" he said.

Her answer came back swiftly. "I've had a ride. I've seen every tree and hill and canyon within twenty miles of the ranch. I'm tired of it."

"There's town," he offered with thinly held patience. "We could take the buckboard in tonight."

"Tell me what there is to do in Capricorn. You'll wind up in a saloon drinking or playing poker with some of your friends while I'll be left sitting in a rocker in the hotel lobby."

Raines's face settled into heavy, grave lines. "There's no pleasing you." Then, as Raines's gaze dropped to the red bow of her mouth, a sudden wild humming shot through him. He took a rapid step toward her. He hooked an arm around Melody's shoulders and pulled her close. He ducked his head to kiss her. At the last instant she turned away and took his kiss on her cheek.

"I can do without that," she murmured, pushing away from him.

Raines scowled. "So you've shown me in the last few weeks." His eyes shone like black polished beads. "That's something you and I will have to thrash out soon."

Melody said nothing. But she was thinking that she couldn't stand much more of Tom Raines. At first his clumsy love-making had intrigued her. But she had soon tired of him. The mere touch of his fingers on her naked flesh sent shivers of revulsion rippling along her skin.

She told herself with bitter regret that she had married an old man. As she drifted away from Raines she found her attention more and more absorbed by the Chevron foreman, Dave Flood. There was something dynamic and compelling about him. The rawhide cut of his body—the broad shoulders, the thin tapering waist, and the blunt angles his jaw made, the firm line of his mouth, the solid strike of his level blue eyes had caught Melody's imagination at once. And if he showed her only the meager attentions that range courtesy decreed, it made him all the more desirable in her eyes.

Now Melody waited stolidly for Raines to pursue the subject of her aloofness to him. But he surprised her by turning away, his keen eyes scanning the far slope beyond the front yard. Two riders had crested the low ridge and now drummed toward them.

"There's Nell and Hoot Ellison," Raines said.

"But where's Dave?" Melody asked quickly.

He craned a sharp look at her, then said, "We'll soon find out."

Together they walked around the side of the ranch house, taking up their station near the veranda. Nell and Ellison came up swiftly on horses that showed the marks of long and hard riding. Before they swung down from the saddle, Raines thrust his question at Nell: "Where's the rest of the outfit?"

"We left Whip Anders and Chuck Ryerson in Blue Mesa," said Nell as she dismounted.

"What about Dave?" Melody asked.

Nell flipped her a tight glance. "I thought you'd ask about him."

Melody reddened and anger stained her eyes. Raines looked at her quizzically, then said to Nell: "Get on with it. Whatever it is you have to say I reckon I won't like it."

"You can count on that," Hoot Ellison broke in. "Dave's pulled a rotten double-cross on the

Chevron and you're out every cent of that trail herd money!"

The weather wrinkles in Raines's face deepened. "Damn it, Hoot, this is no time for fooling."

"He's dead serious," snapped Nell, and proceeded to outline what had happened in Blue Mesa.

When she had finished Raines took off his hat and slammed it to the ground. "By God!" he raged. "That puts the Chevron in a nasty spot. Those were all prime steers. We'll be hard put to get together another bunch like that."

"Even if we did," Ellison pointed out, "we probably would be too late for the market. The current price of fifty dollars per head won't hold much longer."

"Don't I know it!" said Raines. His eyes curdled with fury. "That damned Flood! I took him for a good man—a man I could trust."

"Ask yourself how much any of us really know about him," Nell suggested. "The answer is not a thing."

"You're being unfair," objected Melody.

"Unfair when a man carrying a fortune in cash belonging to his employer conveniently gets himself robbed?" said Nell hotly.

"You don't know that," insisted Melody, an odd catch in her voice.

"What does it look like?" Nell drove her words

at the other girl. "First Dave meets three old friends—gunmen if I ever saw one. He won't talk about them. That night he is robbed. Does he get any of the men who attacked him? No. And for a man who can fight as I've seen him fight that in itself is strange. Then there's a bank robbery. Four men were involved. Dave and the same three men. That's enough for me."

Melody straightened, her face showing a ruddy flash of color. "I still don't believe it. He could have been telling the truth when he said he tried to stop the other men."

Raines whirled on Melody. "You seem mighty disposed to defend Flood," he said.

"What if I am?" Melody asked defiantly.

"He's a man," said Nell with emphasis.

"I don't get your meaning, Nell," Raines said.

"You will—someday."

Raines looked from Melody to Nell and back again. He caught the flare of animosity between the two women, and a knowing light crept into his eyes.

"Don't forget the Chevron belongs to me," Raines told Melody. "And you're part of the Chevron."

"Does that mean I've got to think the same as you?"

Raines bent to retrieve his hat. He dusted it off with his shirt sleeve and replaced it on his head. He said very carefully, "Since you're so interested, I'm giving orders to every Chevron puncher to shoot Flood on sight."

Melody stiffened. A thin smile wreathed Nell's face. Then it vanished as she turned to Raines. "Meanwhile, there's the question of getting another herd together. It's the only way you have of raising cash to pay off your notes."

Raines nodded. "You're right. Reckon I'll take a ride up to the Wind River line camp and see about starting another beef gather." He broke off to send a loud call to Hoot Ellison, who had wandered off to the corral with the horses he and Nell had ridden from Blue Mesa. "Hoot, saddle a couple of fresh horses. We're riding out!"

The puncher waved an arm to signal that he had heard, then ducked back into the corral. Within ten minutes he returned with a couple of strong bays.

"What about Flood?" Ellison demanded.

Raines grabbed the bridle of the bigger of the two bays. He stuck his left boot into the stirrup, then heaved his weight into the saddle. "Nothing we can do about him now," he said to Ellison. "If he's got any sense he'll head for the higher Tetons. Much as I'd like to dab a loop around him, there's more important work to be done right here."

Without another word he sank his spurs into his bay's flanks and galloped out of the yard. Ellison shot after him.

Melody turned her back on the riders and walked up the steps to the veranda. She crossed it to the front door. She heard Nell come up the stairs at her heels, but she moved on into the huge, crudely furnished room that took up half the width of the house without waiting for the other girl.

A great stone fireplace occupied most of one wall. Directly above it hung a soot-stained deer head. There was a wide sofa, two easy chairs, a square table in the middle of the room with a lamp on it, and a colorful Indian blanket covered a wide section of the wall above the sofa.

Melody was close to the table when Nell stopped in the doorway and said, "I hope that Blue Mesa posse catches up with Dave."

Melody spun around. Her thoughts behind frightened eyes were restless and driven. "I hope Dave gets away," she retorted.

Nell came on into the room. There was a narrowed, calculating look in her eyes. "You've got a man, Melody. Or did you forget?"

"I like Dave," Melody said.

"So I've noticed." Nell's voice was thinly edged with malice. "You'd like to get your hooks in him. But time has run out. You'll have to look somewhere else."

Melody felt little tongues of angry fire sweep all over her body. "Someday you'll say too much."

"I'm thinking of Tom," said Nell. "You're not giving him a square deal. I've seen you play up to Dave and others. But Tom isn't the fool you think he is."

"Why don't you tell him?" Melody flared.

"I figure he'll find you out himself before long." All the disturbance that Dave's shocking betrayal had turned loose in Nell now drove her to hammer at Melody, for in Melody's marriage to Tom Raines she saw still another kind of betrayal. "You've discovered that being the wife of Tom Raines wasn't the bargain you anticipated, haven't you? I can see how it must have looked like a good thing. The Chevron's a big outfit and the idea of being Mrs. Tom Raines probably sounded good to you. But it's all rather dull, isn't it? Tom's set in his ways. He's the kind of man that buries himself in his work. That doesn't leave much time for a woman."

"Shut up!" said Melody. Her voice was almost a shout. She advanced menacingly toward the younger girl. "One more word from you and I'll smash some of those pretty teeth down your throat."

Nell was shocked by Melody's outburst. It occurred to her then how vicious her own attack on Melody had been. And she was honest enough with herself to realize that she had struck out at Melody in a sort of senseless retaliation for her own emotional hurts. All during the ride from

Blue Mesa she had refused to acknowledge the depth of her feeling for Flood. The swift tide of events in the railhead town had hit her hard. Bewildered by Flood's apparent defection, she had taken blind refuge in anger. She had not hesitated to brand Flood as a lawbreaker. And she had been alive with the crazy urge to see him brought to heel.

But now she experienced her bitter moment of regret and fear. Now she admitted what she wouldn't have admitted at any time before—that her feeling for Flood was something she couldn't toss aside. He was still deep inside her.

Suddenly Nell could no longer tolerate being in the same room with Melody. She fled across the hall and vanished into the far wing of the house.

After she had gone Melody, still tense and overwrought, strode up and down the room. Nell's barbed shafts had struck home. She didn't love Raines. Whatever her original feeling for Raines had been she doubted if it could be called love. She hated the ranch and the dull routine that marked each successive day. At times she wished she could get away. But there was no place to go.

She stopped before the side window. A stir of movement in the distant trees caught her attention. The figure of a running man approached the house. Melody stifled a cry of surprise and hurried to the door.

# Seven

AFTER crossing Little Teton Creek, Flood put the racing roan on a course that would take him around the flanks of the other trail herd that had been sharing the wide stretch of prairie bunch grass with the Chevron Herefords.

He had almost completed a circle around the herd before the few punchers idling in camp became aware of the fact that he was the object of a man hunt. Then shouts from the hard-riding posse and a few random gunshots spun the lounging rannies into action. At that they were too late. The roan had its head and was traveling at a clip that few range horses could have matched.

Though the trail drivers fell in ahead of the posse, they could not get within rifle range of the speeding roan. The chase carried over the hump of the first low ridge overlooking the town of Blue Mesa and continued on across a six-mile stretch of level prairie. Not once during that grim and grueling test did the roan slacken its headlong pace.

Flood rode with his body bent low, his knees hugging the horse's heaving flanks directly behind and below the withers. They didn't gain on their pursuers. But, by the same token, the posse was unable to close the gap between them.

The race continued in that fashion until Flood struck the first edges of the hills. A scattering of trees and brush began to appear, none of it thick enough to harbor a fleeing rider.

The roan took the first few grades without a tremor. But after another furious two miles the animal's flying gait began to slacken. And when Flood started up the next slope he detected a slight falter in the roan's stride. A thin frown of worry puckered Flood's brow. He realized he'd have to slow down, give the weary animal a chance to blow. At the same time, however, he was reasonably certain that the mounts of the posse were not faring any better.

When he reached the crest of the knoll he swung quickly to the ground and loosened the roan's cinch. A slight ring of white foam rimmed the animal's muzzle. Its sleek, sweat-streaked flanks heaved mightily, the great ribs flaring in and out beneath the taut skin.

A glance behind Flood revealed nothing. The hill he had just climbed and the mile-long stretch of level ground beyond it were empty. He waited there a minute or two. Then the head and shoulders of a rider appeared on the far flank of the ridge Flood had crossed a few minutes before. Close behind the rider came others. They tipped down the slope with a wild yell as they caught sight of their quarry.

Flood moved to the roan. He thrust his shoulder

against the animal's side, pulled the cinch tight, and got into the saddle. Once more the grim chase was resumed.

He shoved the roan down the grade before him. At the bottom he struck out at a gallop. But now he held the roan in a trifle, letting the animal run but not forcing the pace.

Ten minutes went by. When he scanned his back trail again he found that the leaders of the posse had drawn to within a half-mile of his position. The frown on Flood's face deepened. He had expected his pursuers' mounts to fold up. But it wasn't working out that way.

Another hill loomed up. The roan took it at a canter. They gained the top. The roan was faltering again. Flood pushed on grimly. The ridge top was a half mile wide. He was almost across when the first posseman cleared the crest. The man lashed his horse into a gallop. The animal lunged ahead a few paces, then suddenly collapsed, throwing its rider to the ground. Seconds later a second pursuer appeared, his mount going at a labored trot that told Flood the animal was not far from foundering.

It was then that Flood knew he was safe. The posse members had punished their horses too severely. The fierce pace of the hunt had finally taken its toll. The two riders in the lead had virtually ridden their horses into the ground.

Flood pushed on at a canter. He was certain

now that he could draw away from the posse as he pleased. Besides, the country was growing rougher. Trees and brush became more plentiful. Soon he would be in heavy timber and could really set about losing his pursuers.

For the next half-hour he nursed the roan carefully along. On the steeper grades he dismounted and led the gelding to the top before getting into the saddle again. On the level stretches he let the roan proceed at a steady, ground-eating canter.

When he reached the timber he cut into a narrow trace that threaded a brown path through the dim aisle of trees. It wound down to a mountain creek, and Flood turned the roan into the stream, following its twisting course upstream for several miles. Pulling out on rocky ground, he traveled along a shaly bench for several hundred yards before the trees closed around him again.

Only then did he drop from the roan, loosen the cinch again, and give the winded animal the rest it had earned. He threw himself down on a soft carpet of pine needles and took his ease. Now and then, as he rested, he listened for sounds of pursuit. But nothing broke the stillness of the timber.

After an hour Flood resumed his flight. Wherever it was possible, he kept to the cover of trees. The afternoon grew hot. Except for a white scarf of clouds in the southwest the sky was blue and clear. A breeze came out of the west but it, too, was warm and scented with the breath of sage and dry dust.

Sundown brought him to a fork in the narrow trail he had been following. The left-hand fork led to the higher fastnesses of the Teton Mountains where he was sure Calloway and the others had gone. Though Flood's intention of searching for them remained unchanged, another more immediate problem confronted him.

It was early morning since he had eaten. Now, after the long and arduous flight from the Blue Mesa posse, the pressing wants of his stomach made themselves known to him in a slow, grinding ache. He could forego supper without too much hardship. But to face a second day without food was out of the question. And his hunt through the Tetons for Calloway was not likely to be a short one. It might be days, even weeks, before he found Calloway's camp in the labyrinth of hills and canyons and arroyos that studded the Tetons. True, there was fresh game to be brought down with a rifle. But on a man hunt such as he contemplated it would be foolhardy to advertise his presence by indiscriminate shooting.

Gazing out over the rolling, chaparral-studded country that stretched north of him, Flood realized that only two sources of food were open to him. One was the town of Capricorn which he estimated to be about fifteen miles from his present position. Yet Capricorn presented too great a risk. By this time Sheriff Stack of Blue Mesa would have alerted Sheriff Marv Blackwell of Capricorn to be on the lookout for him. In fact, Blackwell might have thrown a posse of his own into the hills in a move to block Flood to the north.

With Capricorn out of the question there was only the Chevron left. That, too, offered a considerable element of peril. He would find no welcome at the Raines outfit now. The Chevron owner would have every one of his hands gunning for him. Yet, at the moment, it was nearer to his own position and seemed to be the lesser of two evils.

Once he had reached this decision, Flood set about making a dry camp in the shelter of some trees well off the beaten trail. He had no saddle roll or blanket so he had to sleep on the ground. But it was not the first time he had done so, and his need for rest was too acute for him to be particularly concerned about his comfort.

In the morning he set out straight for the Chevron. Hunger made its increasing demand on all his senses. At times he felt faintly lightheaded. The emptiness in his belly gnawed sharply at his nerves.

He avoided all the regular cattle trails, not wanting to meet any Chevron punchers. By midmorning he reached a low ridge that gave him a clear view of the ranch and its scattering of corrals and barns. From the cover of a prickly-pear thicket he watched a couple of the Chevron hands ride out. He was too far away to identify the riders, but there was no mistaking the figures of Nell and Melody standing by the veranda.

Seeing both girls told him that Nell had returned. And if he guessed right, she had probably made the return trip from Blue Mesa with Hoot Ellison. As he watched he saw the girls turn and go into the house.

Flood put the roan into motion, circling along the ridge until he got close enough to the headquarters building to quarter down the slope toward the yard.

The Chevron riders were still visible far across the prairie as they started up a slight rise of wooded ground. Then Flood forgot about them and directed his attention to the ranch yard. He studied the bunkhouse, the barn, and corrals for sign of other riders for several minutes until he was sure that Nell and Melody were alone.

That simplified matters. He wouldn't have to burn any powder to get food. Having worked with the Chevron hands for a long time, he didn't relish fighting with any of them to carry through his own private mission of vengeance.

He realized he could expect some opposition from Nell. Recalling the precipitate way he had left her in Blue Mesa and knowing how hot-tempered she was, the outlook in that direction was not a happy one.

But time was running short, and it was this or nothing. So he led the roan down to the very edge of the brush and left him ground-hobbled. Then he scanned the yard once more and made a dash for the house.

He mounted the veranda steps quickly, pulled open the front door, and collided with Melody in the hall as she was hurrying to meet him. Instinctively he grabbed her to keep her from falling. Her arms went around him. Her face, bright and shining with excitement, tipped upward, and suddenly she pulled his head down and kissed him.

There was passion in the kiss and passion in the bold thrust of Melody's body against the long, muscular length of him. He felt her tremble, felt her fingers digging into the flesh at the back of his neck. Fire ran a streak of living flame through him. His shoulders turned rigid and he had to fight the hot rashness that surged through him like the heavy beat of a drum.

He pushed her away almost roughly, his hands clutching her upper arms in an iron grip. Melody showed him a face that was surprised and a little hurt. "Don't you like me to kiss you?" she asked.

It was an awkward moment for Flood. He felt the uneven pounding of blood in his veins. Melody was capable of upsetting any man if she wanted to. The long, ardent kiss she had given him was like a spark touching off the tinder box of his own explosive emotions.

"A man would be a fool if he didn't like to be kissed by you," Flood told her in a voice so gruff he hardly recognized it. "But we've hardly the right to—"

Melody interrupted. "It's Nell you're thinking of."

"And Tom," he added.

"Forget about them. Think about us."

Flood colored under the fierce emphasis of her talk. She drew close. Her eyes probed his bruised features with a strange, unaccountable ardor. Flood felt sweat seeping from the pores of his palms. It wasn't easy to anchor his hands at his sides when Melody so obviously wanted him to take her in his arms.

"Melody," he said finally, "I haven't much time. I—"

Again she broke in. "Dave, you took a terrible chance coming here. Tom is killing wild after what happened in Blue Mesa. He's given the men orders to shoot you on sight."

Flood nodded somberly. "Can't say I blame him under the circumstances. Was that Tom I saw ride off a few minutes ago?"

"Yes. Tom and Hoot Ellison. They went to see about starting another beef gather. That trail herd money you lost is going to be missed."

"I'm sorry about that." Grayness pulled at his

cheeks. His blue eyes were bleak. "You've heard what happened in Blue Mesa, but I want you to know that I had nothing to do with either affair— the stealing of the trail herd cash or the bank robbery."

Melody smiled up at him. "I never thought you did. I tried to tell Nell and Tom that it's not in you to do anything like that."

"Thanks. I'm glad you trust me, Melody." His face tightened as he wondered what she would say if she knew that he was actually an escaped convict from Yuma Prison. Then he said, "What I really stopped off at the Chevron for was food. A man on the dodge from the law has to eat."

Melody thrust herself against him. Her smooth oval cheeks puckered with concern. "Of course, Dave. Take whatever you want. Then you'd better head for the Tetons and the country beyond."

"I'm going to the Tetons, but not for the reason you think."

"I don't understand, Dave."

He looked down at her. He was deadly serious and he did not answer her smile in kind. "Melody, I've a pretty good idea who those men in the robbery were." He saw she was about to break in and added, "Don't ask me how or why. I'm sure they'll hole up in the Tetons. I'm going after them."

Melody clutched frantically at him. "Dave, you can't do it alone."

"I can try," he said simply.

"You'll be killed."

Melody's arms went around Flood. She buried her face against his chest. Flood remained immobile, struggling against the impulse to slip his arms around her.

"Tom ought to see you now," said the brittle voice of Nell from the room on the other side of the hall.

Flood and Melody whirled. Flood saw the angry scorn in Nell's eyes. Then he saw the gun steady in her hand, the gleaming barrel pointed at his chest.

"Put up your hands, Dave," she ordered. "This is the mate of the gun you took from me in Blue Mesa. I can assure you it's loaded."

"Nell, you fool!" said Melody. "Throw that gun away." She started toward Nell.

"Hold it, Melody," Nell snapped. "Stay right where you are."

Melody stopped. There was no mistaking the determination in Nell's tone. Flood half lifted his arms.

"Nell," he said, "you've got to believe me. I had no part in that holdup. I blundered into it and tried to stop it."

Nell sneered. "It looked like it, all right, with one of your gun-slick friends trying to hoist you aboard his horse when your roan spooked up."

Flood's retort was sharp. "They did that to make it appear I was with them."

"Why would they do that?" Nell demanded.

"Never mind why."

Nell nodded, her face still tight and stubborn. "You've taken us all for a passel of fools. That's finished. You won't go any farther than this room." She retreated to the doorway. "This time you won't have the opportunity to use me as a shield."

"You have my apology for that," Flood told her. "But I had to get away. I couldn't risk being thrown in jail."

"But you could risk having me shot."

Flood's face turned dark, the muscles controlled and quiet. Nell had never appeared more beautiful to him. Her anger lent color to her cheeks and whipped a frosty fire in her cool eyes.

"There's nothing I can say to that," he admitted. "You're right about that." He shrugged his shoulders in a gesture of resignation. "What are you going to do?"

"Hand you over to the sheriff."

Melody cut in with a swift, rash anger. "Not if I can stop you."

The two girls faced each other across a few feet of space. The threat of violence stretched a taut, invisible string between them. Melody's long and full upper lip flattened out. Her eyes grew dangerously bright.

Nell felt the insidious pressure of Melody's antagonism. It beat against her like a cold, unfriendly wind. Then her voice jarred out a curt warning. "Stay out of this, Melody, or you'll get hurt."

"I don't care," said Melody. "Dave is innocent. I'm sure of it. He told me."

Nell's lip curled. "He told you. And you believe him."

Flood, watching the two girls and seeing the ugly hostility that whirled between them, knew that he had to step in. In Nell's present mood she was perfectly capable of putting a bullet in Melody if the other girl charged her. They were both riding their tempers. A word or a gesture would touch them off.

Deliberately he took a step toward Nell. "Put down your gun, Nell. I came here for some food then I'm off for the Tetons to catch up with those gun-slicks you insist on thinking are my friends."

"Stay back," said Nell. Her hand stiffening around the handle of the .38 was white and hard.

Head bowed, shoulders hunched, his whole manner indomitable, Flood moved on toward Nell. "Put it down," he said.

Nell's eyes narrowed. A tiny muscle at the base of her throat began to throb. She wiggled the gun in her hand. She said hoarsely, "Come one more step and I'll shoot!"

The rustling rasp of death quaked in the abrupt

stillness that filled the house. A cold brightness pulsed in Flood's eyes. Nell's breathing was suddenly loud and uneven. Trouble was ready to burst loose in the room, and the certainty of it turned Flood completely reckless. His nerves were stretched to the breaking point. He looked at the unwavering barrel of Nell's gun and set himself for a quick dive at her.

Then Tom Raines's booming voice filled the air.

"It's all right, Nell! I'll do any shooting that's necessary."

He had gained the veranda without being detected. Now he opened the door and shoved his six-foot three frame into the hall. He had his Colt fisted and his gray eyes were utterly without mercy.

"Good work, Nell," he said. Then he levered his heavy glance at Flood. "Your roan didn't stay ground-tied in the brush or you might have gotten away again. I saw the critter from the top of a ridge and a funny hunch made me come back."

Melody was white and shaken with fear. She saw the murder lust in her husband's face and threw her hands out to him in frantic appeal. "Tom, you must let Dave go. He didn't—"

"Let him go?" repeated Raines incredulously. "You're out of your mind. This damned sidewinder has put the Chevron in a tight we may never get out of." As he talked the rancher's voice gained in volume and fury. There were dark puffs under his eyes and his mouth was a flinty, thinly drawn wedge against the stormy malevolence of his face. The gun in his hand shifted, then grew rock-steady. He threw a savage question at Flood. "You got anything to say before I plant a forty-five slug in the middle of your guts?"

Flood's stomach muscles churned into a knot. Death was a frigid whisper in the air. Nell caught her breath and eyed her uncle with startled surprise. But it was Melody who precipitated the rush of action that followed.

The black-haired girl uttered a wild cry. She picked up a heavy metal ash tray from the table and flung it at Raines. The rancher saw the missile coming and tried to duck. He was just a bit too late. The thick-based tray struck him high along the side of the head. He fell forward, and as he fell his gun sent a bullet crashing into the ceiling.

Flood lunged at Raines, angling for the Colt which skittered along the floor as the rancher measured his length on the puncheons. Then Flood remembered Nell. He whirled around. Nell's .38 was swinging around to cover him. He didn't know whether she would shoot or not and somehow he didn't care. He stepped over Raines and threw himself at Nell.

But Melody was a fraction of a second ahead of him. She struck Nell with the tip of one shoulder.

A swinging arm smashed Nell's gun wrist and knocked the .38 from her fingers. In a moment the two girls were locked in a furious struggle, biting and clawing at each other.

"Dave!" Melody cried, her voice muffled against Nell's breast. "Take what you want from the kitchen before Ellison comes back!"

Flood hesitated, not sure of his next move. The two girls were wrestling around the room. They fell against the table, upending it. Arms locked around each other, they pitched on top of the table, then rolled to the floor in a snarl of arms and legs. Suddenly Melody wrenched free, groped for Nell's .38 just a few inches from her fingers. With a rapid lunge she gripped it in her hand and rose. Then, pushing a strand of fallen hair away from her eyes, she leveled the weapon at Nell.

"Get up!" she ordered curtly.

Blood seeped from a long scratch on Nell's left cheek. There was a ruddy bruise at the tip of her chin. She glared at Melody but got to her feet.

Flood sent one last appeal to Nell. "Will you listen to me now?"

Nell waved him away. "You'd better get out while you still have the chance," she advised him, her features showing him no quarter.

"Go ahead, Dave!" Melody urged. "Any moment now Hoot Ellison may come rushing in to see what's keeping Tom."

"All right." There was a dull finality in Flood's voice.

He shot a keen glance out the doorway. The yard was still empty, but it might not be empty long. Even so, he paused to drop down beside Tom Raines. The rancher was breathing heavily. The heavy ash tray had raised a big lump on the side of his head and had broken the skin in one small area. He would probably be on his feet in another ten minutes with only a headache to remind him of what had occurred.

Flood hurried out to the kitchen. The pantry shelves were well stocked with food staples. He helped himself to generous quantities of flour, bacon, beans, and coffee, and even appropriated a coffeepot and a small frying pan. He stuffed the things in two cloth sacks, then returned to the front room where Melody was still standing guard over Nell.

"Thanks, Melody, for your help," he said.

She gave him a warm smile that was mixed with fear.

"Be careful, Dave," she said. "I'll be thinking of you."

But Flood's attention had already gone past her and come to rest upon Nell. He paused briefly in the doorway, waiting for some sign of relenting in Nell. No change stirred the controlled quiet of her features. And her eyes when they touched his were remote and distant.

Flood's shoulders settled in a dismal, rounded line and he wheeled through the doorway. Once outside he skirted the side of the house quickly. He saw that the roan had drifted out of the shelter of the trees and was munching a few tufts of dry grass in the yard.

The clatter of hoofs somewhere beyond him, on the far side of the house, drove him into a run. He reached the gelding, stuffed the food in one saddlebag and the two pans in the other. Then he jumped aboard and spurred the roan back through the trees.

Flood had hardly been gone three minutes when Hoot Ellison halted his horse in the front yard and dropped to the ground. He rushed up the veranda steps and burst into the front room just as Tom Raines was staggering to his feet.

"What happened?" Ellison blurted.

One gnarled hand rubbing the bruise on the side of his head, Raines growled his reply. "Flood was here—but he got away, thanks to my wife." Raines whirled on Melody. One savage blow of his fist knocked the gun out of her hand. "I won't forget this," he fumed. "You'll never interfere in my affairs again. Get to your room."

For a moment Melody felt her legs turn to water. It was as if she had become boneless. Her body was a cold mass of quaking jelly. Raines looked thoroughly wild. He stood over her with the muscles bunched in his hairy arms, the knuckles in his huge hands standing out like knots. She thought for a moment he meant to strangle her. She felt the cords in her neck tighten in panic. The glassy look of hysteria filled her eyes. Then she darted past Raines and fled into the other wing of the house.

"What did Flood want here?" Ellison demanded.

"I reckon you can answer that, Nell," said Raines.

There was a spent and beaten look about the blond girl. Her skin was very white, completely drained of color. She said dully, "He came for food and told the same story about planning to track down the bank robbers up in the Tetons."

"More likely he came here to get food to carry to his friends," grunted Raines.

Nell nodded, pushing the hair away from her face. For some strange reason she wanted to scream. She wanted Raines and Ellison to leave her alone. The scream rose up through her body. She held it back with a supreme effort of will. But it left her throat dry and aching.

Raines stamped around the room, looking for his gun. He located it behind a chair, thrust it back in his holster.

"Come on!" he said to Ellison. "The cattle can wait. We may still have a chance to head Flood off before he gets out of the foothills."

Together the two men clattered out of the room and ran to their horses.

# Eight

THE ten-minute start Flood had in getting away from the Chevron ranch was enough to put him in the clear. Although he heard the dim crash of riders deep in the timber behind him and guessed that Raines and Ellison were hot on his trail, he did not worry about being caught.

The roan was fresh and eager to run. And the timber offered ample cover. On all sides of him thick brush rimmed the trail. The land dipped and rolled to the rough, uneven contours of the hills. Canyons and ravines occasionally broke the pattern of wooded slopes. Once Flood sent the roan slamming through a deep culvert criss-crossed with vines and stunted trees, then climbed steeply along an aspen-lined slope to a high, rocky bench that promised to conceal all signs of his travel.

Twenty minutes after leaving the Chevron he knew he had put Raines and Ellison out of reach. He slackened the pace then, and let the roan go along at an easy canter.

At noon he made a short stop in the lee of a high red butte whose lower slope slanted inward to form a shallow cave. Here in the protection of the rocky overhang he risked a fire and put together a hot meal of bacon and beans and coffee. He ate ravenously and drank a half pot of coffee.

Afterward he killed the fire, scattered the ashes carefully, and raked leaves and dirt over the spot. Then he went back to the roan, mounted, and continued on his way.

He was still in the lower foothills of the Tetons when night fell and he made camp. Once, in the middle of the long afternoon, he sighted a small band of riders in a grassy swale several miles away. They were working toward his position and he guessed that they were a part of the Blue Mesa posse. Flood moved on, striking deeply into the timber. When he next stopped on a high ridge and looked back in the direction he had been traveling he found the country empty of riders.

During the three days that followed he worked steadily higher into the Tetons. He rode with perpetual caution, sticking to cover wherever possible. The air grew colder and rarer but the weather held sunny and clear. A number of times he flushed wild game out of hidden thickets. Though he was tempted to try his luck with the .38 he held his fire, not wishing to advertise his presence in the area.

The search grew steadily more monotonous as the hours wore on. He had no clear idea where Calloway might be likely to take refuge. He was sure it was in the Tetons. But the Tetons spread out over a good piece of country. A man could spend weeks in these scattered hills and canyons without meeting a single rider. And to men seeking to remain concealed it would be relatively easy to avoid detection.

Then, late in the afternoon of the fourth day, Flood sighted a thin column of gray smoke against the blue vault of sky three or four miles above the narrow bench where he had stopped to rest the roan. It was such a thin trickle of smoke that it was barely discernible.

Flood felt the quickening rush of blood in his veins. That the smoke came from a campfire he had no doubt. But he couldn't be sure who the fire belonged to. It might be the camp of some posse hunting him. Or it might be the mountain hideout of Calloway, Trotter, and Rickard. Having come this far, however, Flood meant to investigate.

Since the smoke came from a hidden ridge above him, he pulled immediately into the brush and started on a wide circle that would bring him to the distant knoll from another quarter.

Twenty minutes later he halted at the foot of a wooded slope. Above him, winding through the closely growing trees, was a narrow trace. Marks of recent travel were faintly discernible in the earth. Just a wisp of the smoke could be seen now trailing off into the blue vault of sky. The camp was only a few hundred yards away, and he realized that he'd have to go the rest of the distance on foot.

He drew the roan off the trail, proceeding carefully so that noise of his movements would not be carried to the campers. Sixty feet in from the trail he ground-hobbled the roan behind a wide-boled tree. Then he cut diagonally through the brush until he struck the trail again.

Gun in hand, he started the steep climb. The higher up he went the thinner the brush became, until finally he found himself at the rim of a broad bench. It was really a high shelf perched amid a profusion of boulders on three sides. The fourth side he could not see. But as he moved along the last hundred yards through a thin cover of chaparral he noted a break in the wall of rocks to his left.

He paused for a few moments behind a clump of junipers while he sucked air into his lungs. The grade was quite sheer and the climb had taken the wind out of him. The trail here was slightly rocky. Some sharp white scrapes on the shale told of the passage of steel-shod horses. Beyond and above the rock wall the column of smoke was clear and scented with fresh pine.

Waiting there with his heart pumping violently and all senses attuned to the hint of danger, Flood caught the indistinct rumble of voices. It continued sporadically, but he was unable to make any sense out of that low murmuring.

A reckless impatience drove him forward. At a half-run he emerged from his shelter and rushed to the shoulder of rocks that defined the near boundary of the bench. Again he waited, not sure if the sound of his progress up the grade had been heard by those in the camp.

When no alarm followed he slid along the boulder line until he gained the opening. It was scarcely wide enough to allow the passage of two mounted men. He ducked through the aperture and immediately dropped to the ground behind a waist-high wedge of stone that jutted out from the wall close to his right elbow.

Directly ahead of him and just a hundred feet away was the fire that had given off the telltale column of smoke. He could hear the crackling of the flames and the scent of pine was stronger. Added to that scent was the pungent aroma of boiling coffee.

Around the fire two men were seated. One swift glance had shown Flood that he had come to the right place. And it was his good fortune that both men had their backs partially to the opening in the rocks or he would have been discovered at once.

Bill Calloway was hunkered on the right side of the fire. He gripped a tin mug of coffee in his big fist, his attention on Ed Trotter who was leaning toward the charred brown pot that held the brew. Across from them, on the far side of the fire, two saddle horses were grazing. A set of bulging saddlebags lay on the ground close to one of the animals.

Flood guessed that the money he'd come for was in those saddlebags. One thing bothered him, however. There were only two horses. There should have been three unless Nap Rickard had ridden off somewhere. He had no wish to rush Calloway and Trotter and then find himself caught from the rear by the sudden arrival of Rickard. Accordingly, he elected to delay his attack for a moment until he was able to size up his surroundings.

He saw that the camp was formed in the shape of a big bowl. Scattered boulders shut in most of three sides of the bowl although there were some stunted pine trees and a few other bushes growing near the rocks. On the fourth side, well beyond the grazing horses, there were no rocks—just a thick line of trees shelving downward and out of sight.

Flood's eyes swung back to Trotter, who had filled his mug with coffee and now set the pot back on the flames. The stocky, thin-lipped outlaw spoke to Calloway in a gruff voice in which there was a trace of caustic humor. "I wonder how your friend Flood is making out."

Calloway grinned evilly. His heavy upper lip twisted. "I reckon he's perched in a cell in the Blue Mesa jail waiting to be hung."

"You figure they'll send him back to Yuma?"

"If they find out he's still got time to serve."

Trotter chuckled. "You sure fixed him by making it look like he was trying to make a getaway with us."

Calloway scowled. "That was for horning in on our game. We made a big haul from that bank, but for a couple of minutes I thought Flood might queer the whole deal."

"Speaking of that haul," said Trotter, "when do we get to spend some of that dinero?"

"Not for a while yet."

Trotter sat up. His face darkened. "Hell, I'm getting tired of staying cooped up in these hills. I'd like a fling in some town. Damn it, you realize we haven't even got a bottle of whisky?"

"You'll have plenty of time to celebrate," said Calloway. "I want to be sure there are no law dogs creeping around the Tetons when we bust out of here."

"We've been camped here almost a week. By this time that posse from Blue Mesa is back home." Trotter swallowed the rest of his coffee then flung the mug down. "As for me, if Rickard isn't back by dawn tomorrow I'm taking some of my share of the loot and heading over the mountains to Great Forks for a little hoorawing."

"Like hell you are!" growled Calloway. "I'm running this show. We'll move out of here when I say so. Not before."

From his hiding place behind the waist-high rock Flood watched the two renegades glare at each other. Trotter tensed while his thin lips skinned back against his yellow teeth. Calloway remained relatively calm except for the hardening of his jaw line.

Trotter said nothing more. Gradually the tension went out of him. Then Calloway spoke again. "I've got a couple of other things rigged up for us before we pull up stakes. We'll need the men Rickard is rounding up."

"That's something else I don't like," said Trotter. "Three of us are enough. I'm not cutting anyone else into my share of the loot."

"You won't have to. That money we got from Flood and from the bank gets out just three ways. The men Rickard is bringing in will help us on a few big cattle deals."

"Cattle deals? What are you talking about?"

Calloway laughed at Trotter's puzzlement. "There are two or three well-stocked ranches in the Teton foothills. Among them are Sam Hurst's Sun ranch and the Chevron outfit that Flood works for. Both outfits are operating with just a handful of riders. If we play things right we ought to be able to run off a good hunk of their beef and take the critters right across the state line. It'll take extra men to handle the critters. That's where Rickard's friends come in. After we've grabbed the beef we want we'll clear out and Rickard's bunch can go back where they came from."

Suddenly Flood decided he had heard all he needed to know. The money was there in plain sight. Rickard was away from camp and the time to strike was right now before Rickard returned with reinforcements.

Already the sun was sinking behind the distant western spires of the Tetons. Long bands of orange and red light streaked the sky. In all the hidden pockets of the rugged mountain stringers deep shadows began to form. A stiff breeze sprang up, riffling the treetops.

Flood stepped out from the sheltering wedge of rock. He took five steps toward the fire before Calloway jerked his head around and noticed him.

"Freeze! Both of you!" Flood snapped, the short-barreled .38 steady in his hand.

Trotter lurched to one side, started to go for his gun.

"Hold it!" said Flood, still pacing forward.

The stocky outlaw's hand dropped. Calloway regarded Flood with a look of shocked unbelief.

"I reckon you gents didn't expect to see me so soon again," Flood said. He smiled humorlessly. It was a smile that stretched his lips but failed to reach the cold steel of his eyes. "Your plan to leave me trapped in Blue Mesa didn't work, Calloway. Too bad—for you. Get on your feet—both of you."

Calloway and Trotter rose slowly from their position around the fire. With Flood watching them intently, they unbuckled their gun belts at his sharp command and let them slide to the ground.

"Where is it?" Flood asked.

"I don't know what you're talking about," grumbled Calloway.

"Never mind," said Flood. "I reckon it's in those saddlebags." Calloway gave a slight, betraying start. Flood went on, "From what I heard back there in the rocks, you fellows didn't have a chance to spend any of the money. I'm taking the whole business—the Chevron trail herd cash and the loot from the bank."

Calloway's face turned gray and flinty. He stared long and hard at the gun in Flood's fist. At last he said heavily, "I'll cut you in for a fourth of the money."

"What the hell for?" demanded Trotter, standing with his shoulders hunched and his arms crooked at the elbows as if he were ready to spring at Flood.

"Shut up!" shouted Calloway. "Let me handle this." To Flood he said, "How about it?"

Flood's answer was abrupt and flat. "It's no deal. The Chevron money goes to Tom Raines and the cash from the bank goes back to Blue Mesa. I aim to see that delivery is made."

"You fool!" said Calloway. "Don't you know they'll toss you in the calaboose whether you go back to Blue Mesa with the money or not?"

"I'll risk it." Flood's cheeks were firm and controlled. "You put the outlaw brand on me in that town. I'm going back to take it off.

113

Meanwhile, here's a little warning. Stay out of my way—both of you. The next time we meet come smoking!"

"By God, I will!" shouted Calloway. His face swelled with rage while his skin took on a queer mottled hue. "I'll pay you back. I'll hound you from hell to breakfast."

The shadows of dusk deepened along the high ramparts of the Tetons. Slowly the faint gray light in the sky faded.

Flood waved his gun at the saddlebags. "Calloway, bring those saddlebags over here."

Calloway stood immobile by the fire.

"Hurry!" snapped Flood. "I haven't much time." He eared back the hammer of the .38 to full cock.

Calloway growled a curse, but he trudged over to the edge of the brush. Flood moved closer to the fire, his attention equally divided between Calloway and Trotter. He saw Calloway reach the saddlebags and bend down to pick them up.

Suddenly the big renegade whirled around. His hand, dropping to the bags, plunged into one of the pouches and reappeared with a long-barreled .45.

Flood flung himself to the right, landing in a half-sprawl as Calloway squeezed off a hasty shot. Propped on one elbow, Flood sent a lead charge through Calloway's shoulder. The outlaw reeled. He dropped his weapon and went down.

Simultaneously Trotter dived for the Colt at his feet. Flood fired once and missed. Then Trotter got his fingers around his gun and dropped hammer on a shot that whined within inches of Flood's face.

Flood rolled and came to his feet in a low crouch.

Trotter was up, too, an ugly snarl tugging at his mouth. Flood saw the renegade's weapon chop down into line. Quickly he swung the .38 around and fired all in one blur of motion.

The two shots seemed to come in one drum-roll of sound. But actually Flood's bullet exploded from the bore of the .38 a fraction of a second before Trotter's slug was sent on its way. That slim margin of time was the gap between life and death for both men.

Flood's bullet drilled the center of Trotter's forehead while dust spurted up beneath Flood's boots from the skittering impact of Trotter's errant shot. Immediately afterward a blue hole appeared in Trotter's forehead and he pitched forward. He was dead when he hit the ground.

But Flood had already turned away from Trotter to watch Calloway scrambling to his feet and pitching another shot at him. The bullet slapped at Flood's holster in passing and ripped the leather away. Flood felt his belt drop and slide down around his hips. It threw him off balance. He ducked his head and Calloway's third slug missed him by scant inches, droning over the spot where his head had been.

Struggling to stay on his feet, Flood squeezed off a fast shot, aimed low. Calloway jolted to a stop. It was as if he had run into an invisible wall. His left leg collapsed under him. He cursed in pain. Some powerful drive of his will pulled him up again. Dark blood was already staining his pants leg. He reeled forward, firing wildly until his gun hammer clicked on an empty chamber. He was close to the fire when his leg folded under him. Hands outflung, he tried to break his fall, tried to twist away from the blaze. But the energy had drained out of him and his long body crashed into the flames, sending up a shower of sparks.

A shrill scream of agony ripped from Calloway's throat. He writhed in the flaring red blaze. The smell of scorched clothing filled the air. Flood raced forward. He reached down for one of Calloway's outstretched arms and hauled him from the fire. Then he ripped the smoldering shirt from the outlaw's back and beat out a circle of flames that had started along the back of one pants leg.

Hunkered there beside Calloway, he caught the odor of singed skin. The flesh of one cheek was seared. The eyebrow was gone and some of the hair had been burned away from the edge of his forehead.

Flood experienced a sick revulsion of feeling.

He looked once at the motionless shape of Trotter. There was no pleasure in killing a man. Under the stress of anger or danger Flood could whip himself to sheer and savage violence. In those moments he was hard and implacable, welcoming the reek of burnt powder, the crashing explosion of gunshots. In those moments he was a man with hell in his heart and hell in his holsters.

But now that the shooting was all over he felt strangely hollow and empty. Horror was an acrid taste in his mouth. He looked at Calloway with cheeks that were ashen and eyes that were dim with regret.

Writhing in pain, red blood from his shoulder wound staining his shirt, and his features a blackened, sooty mass, Calloway shouted hoarsely at Flood. "I'll kill you. Someday I—I'll kill you!"

"You called the play, Bill," Flood told him.

Calloway's swollen mouth twisted as he repeated almost insanely, "I'll kill you!"

Flood crouched beside him, intending to see what he could do for the outlaw's wounds. As his fingers jerked at Calloway's red-soaked underwear, he heard a faint shout off in the distance. At the same time the sound of trampled brush and the hard ring of metal on stone was carried to him by the wind. He realized at once that Rickard must be returning with reinforcements.

One glance at Calloway's pain-racked eyes told him he had guessed correctly. "You're finished," the outlaw gasped. "That's Rickard bringing help. You're a dead huckleberry."

Flood jumped up, shoved the .38 in the waistband of his trousers, and sprinted toward the two saddlers. He caught the reins of a big roan that greatly resembled his own horse and dragged the animal over to the edge of the trees.

The tumult of noise back down the slope became louder and louder. Remembering the narrow trail he had followed up to the bench, he knew he could not possibly break through in that direction. The only way out was through the gap in the brush ahead of him, and there the ground seemed to pitch away in a sheer, unseen precipice.

Near the trees Flood retrieved the saddlebags. He heaved them across the saddle and climbed aboard just as the first rider showed at the wall of rock two hundred feet behind him. He slammed his heels into the roan's flanks. The animal bounded away at a run. Hoofs drummed across the hardpan behind him. Then a gun boomed.

Flood hurtled toward the narrow gap in the trees. The firing behind him increased. Rickard's strident yell boiled across the clearing. Suddenly the roan was at the edge of the glade. Flood's jaw set in a hard line as he sent the horse skidding down the shale-dotted slope. The roan traveled thirty yards at a headlong, stumbling rate then lost its footing and pitched over sideways. Flood was thrown out of the saddle. He struck the shale on one shoulder, spun around once, then plunged into empty space.

# Nine

TOM RAINES was in an ugly mood when he returned to the Chevron ranch with Hoot Ellison after their futile pursuit of Dave Flood. Both men had pushed their saddle ponies hard and they were weary from two hours of steady riding over rugged terrain.

Raines dropped heavily to the ground and handed the reins of his gelding to Ellison. "Take this critter over to the corral, then rope out three fresh horses."

Ellison regarded him quizzically. "Three?"

"Yeah. You heard me."

Raines turned his back on the puncher and stalked up the veranda steps. Ellison shrugged his shoulders and trotted off to the corral to dismount and offsaddle both horses.

Melody was sitting in the big front room idly leafing through the pages of a magazine when the Chevron owner entered. Raines's thin, gray-black eyebrows drew together. He asked gruffly, "Where's Nell?"

"She went off somewhere on that new paint pony of hers," Melody told him without looking up. "She didn't say where she was going—and I didn't ask."

Raines glowered at Melody. "Thought I told you to go to your room."

Melody's cool, unfriendly glance lifted to her husband. "So you did. But if you want me, you see me here."

Raines took off his dusty sombrero and slammed it on the table. "When I tell you to do a thing, I want you to do it," he growled.

"You're not ordering me around as if I were a dog."

"As long as I'm running this ranch you'll do as I say."

Melody flung the magazine to the floor. She stood up, her cheeks quivering and aflame. "I'll not take that kind of talk from you. I'm your wife. Remember?"

Raines hit her savagely with his reply. "See that you remember."

"Explain that remark."

"You understand well enough," muttered Raines. He faced her angrily, his shoulders bent a little, as if he were crouched and ready to spring at her. "Anybody that works for the Chevron owes me his loyalty. I expect the same loyalty from you."

He paused briefly, and Melody said sharply, "Go on. Let's hear the rest of it."

"You know what happened to the Chevron trail herd and you know the man responsible for losing the sale money," Raines said. "I put my trust in Dave Flood and he betrayed me. Yet you deliberately interfered this morning—let him get away when we had him dead to rights."

"Dave was telling the truth," said Melody, the color still high and vivid in her cheeks. "You were ready to kill him."

"He's got a killing coming to him!"

"Not if I can prevent it."

Suspicion darkened Raines's eyes. His voice turned ugly. "Maybe it's time you chose between the Chevron and Dave Flood."

Melody's glance was like a sharp-edged steel weapon. "You've got your gall saying a thing like that," she said.

"I'll say that and more," he responded. "You were ready enough to marry me back in Kansas City. But for the last few weeks you've done nothing but complain. I warned you what ranch life would be like. You made your choice and you're stuck with it. I don't know what there is between you and Dave Flood—"

Raines never finished the remark because Melody stepped close to him and swung the palm of her hand stingingly across his mouth. The blow drove his upper lip against his teeth, slashing the skin.

"There's nothing between us!" Melody raged. "But right now, if there was a chance of it, I'd go to Dave or any other man to get away from you and your ugly suspicions."

She started past Raines, but he pivoted and caught her arm. With a cruel jerk he pulled her back to him. She gasped in pain.

"You're hurting me!" she cried.

Wild emotions ripped through Raines. His face looked black and venomous. "Don't ever hit me again, Melody," he said in a voice so thick that it almost choked him. "If you do, I won't be responsible for what happens."

Looking at Raines, Melody suddenly saw the features of an utter stranger. Rage had completely transformed him. His skin was twisted into horrible wrinkles. His eyes were narrow slits and full of wrath. At that moment she came to fear him.

"Let me go!" she said, turning frantically in his grasp.

She finally wrenched free and backed away from him. A shudder swept her from head to foot. She was breathing rapidly, as if she had been running. She shrank toward the wall, seeming to grow smaller all the time.

Raines paced toward her. He saw her eyes roll in terror and stopped a few feet away. "You spoke of getting out of here," he said, his glance like a steel drill boring through her weak flesh. He pointed to the door behind her. "There's the door. You can go, but if you go don't expect to come back." He stopped abruptly, feeling his anger cool a trifle. She was a beautiful woman. To lose her would be like running a sword through him. Watching the lovely lines of her face, the lush swell of her breasts, he remembered with a deep pang the intimacies they had known. He knew he'd rather tear his heart out than let her go to any other man. But there was too much pride in his nature to back down from the stand he had taken. And so he waited for her answer.

To Melody, Raines's ultimatum came as a tremendous shock. She hadn't imagined that his rage could carry him to such an extremity. He was like a man possessed. Until this moment she'd had her way with him. He'd been thankful for the favors she'd doled out to him. Often, lately, she had laughed secretly at the aching want of her she'd detected in his eyes. The same hunger was mirrored in his glance now, only it was tempered with pride and ungovernable rage.

She knew from the stubborn set of his jaw and the grim pitch of his talk that Raines would not retreat from his position. He was too hardheaded for that. And suddenly Melody experienced another kind of fear—a fear too recent to be unfamiliar. If she left the Chevron she would be giving up all the security and comfort she had won for herself when she married Raines.

There was nothing for her back in Kansas City—and nothing for her anywhere in the state of Wyoming except at the Chevron. Dave Flood could offer her nothing even if he wanted her— which he didn't. Dave was a marked man with a whole range against him. It didn't matter that he stirred her feelings as Raines had never done. It was Raines who could give her the things she valued above everything else.

"I've no intention of going," she told him finally.

Raines's features relaxed slightly. Beads of sweat crept out on his forehead. That had been a near thing. He hid his satisfaction behind a cold, impersonal mask.

"Ellison and I are going up to the Wind River line camp. He's saddling a horse for you."

"All right," she said listlessly.

He waited for Melody to walk past him and out the door. At the corral Ellison had the fresh horses saddled. He greeted Melody but she didn't answer him. He looked from the girl to Raines whose face still showed signs of the ravages of violent emotion. Ellison knew, then, that there had been a showdown of some kind between them.

They swung into their saddles without any attempt being made to ease the tension with idle talk. Once out of the yard they headed north along a narrow wagon road. They left the road after two miles and cut across a serrated line of hills. The sun continued hot, and in the distance heat waves danced against the faded blue background of sky.

They passed isolated bands of Chevron stock grazing in hidden swales or grassy pockets in the hills. Melody didn't pay much attention to the

125

animals, but Raines and Ellison never failed to study them intently as they moved on.

Five miles from the ranch Ellison broke the long, uneasy silence. "That line fence yonder looks as if it's been cut. All three strands are down."

Raines swung his attention toward a barbed-wire barrier that marched up and down the rolling hills as far as Melody could see. The two men spurred away from her. She followed more leisurely. When she reached the fence, both Raines and Ellison had already dismounted and were intently examining the severed strands of wire.

"It's been cut all right," said Raines.

"And here's something else," called Ellison as he wandered away from the fence line. "Looks like a herd of cows has gone through—and not so long ago, either."

Raines hurried over to Ellison. Together they studied the welter of hoofprints that churned up the loose earth a short distance away from the fence.

"Some horse sign here too," observed Raines.

"Which means the critters didn't wander over here by themselves," added Ellison.

"Hell, that cut wire tells you that."

Hoot Ellison rose from the crouched position he had assumed to study the trail sign and said, "You figure Sam Hurst is getting ambitious?"

Raines's tall frame seemed to knot up. Red flecks of temper glinted in his narrowing eyes. "We'll soon see," he said.

"Are you fixing to ride over to the Sun outfit now?"

"Just as soon as we round up those cow critters."

Raines stepped to his horse and mounted. Hoot Ellison followed suit. Raines nodded curtly to Melody. The girl gigged her pony along in their wake.

Fifteen minutes later they came upon a small band of cattle grazing along the gentle slope of a grassy hill. Once more Raines and Ellison spurred ahead of Melody. They circled the edges of the herd, leaning from their saddles to inspect the brands on the animals' flanks.

"It's Sun beef all right," grunted Ellison as he joined Raines.

The Chevron owner nodded grimly. "I count about fifty head." He turned to squint his eyes at the sun. Then he uncoiled a few lengths of rope from the lariat he carried on his saddle horn. "Let's start hazing these critters back where they belong."

Ellison kneed his gelding around and trotted around the far flank of the now restlessly stirring cattle. He slapped the end of his rope against the flanks of a few stragglers at the far side of the glade, while Raines started the bunch moving up in front.

With a couple of loud "Hi-yahs!" the Sun cows swung into motion, a few of them lowing in protest.

"If they'd drifted a few miles farther west they'd have been spotted by the boys at our Wind River camp," said Ellison, once more coming abreast of Raines as the latter sat motionless in the saddle to let the herd drift past.

Raines didn't answer. He watched the cows for a moment or two, then twisted in the saddle to face Melody.

"Come along," he growled. "Maybe you'll learn something about driving cattle. You hold down the left flank and don't let any of the critters stray into the brush behind you."

The command was given gruffly and without a smile. Melody said nothing. She had watched a few cattle drives but had never taken part in any of the actual work. In fact, she had no liking for cattle and was always a little uneasy when riding among them.

However, the Sun Herefords were well fed and watered and they moved along without much urging. Melody was able to keep a safe distance from the nearest cows and still hold down her flank position.

In a short time they reached the gap in the Chevron line fence and hazed the cows through the opening. The ground shelved gently away from the barrier in a long, downhill grade, then lifted again past a series of low ridges. A dry wash sliced across the trail. Raines steered the bunch into the gravel-filled stream bed, followed the winding course for three quarters of a mile before hazing the critters out again on a broad stretch of flats.

Two riders loped out of the trees far to the left and immediately swerved in their direction, coming at a fast gallop.

"Here it comes!" shouted Ellison through the thin curtain of dust that hung over the tail end of the Sun herd. He sank spur steel into the flanks of his horse and sped along the right flank to join Raines.

"I'll do the talking," warned Raines, sliding the gun up and down in his holster to free it of saddle crimp.

Ellison grinned. "But who'll do the shooting?"

"No gunplay unless they start the ball rolling."

"Sure," agreed Ellison, looking to the smooth action of his own .45. "But keep a weather eye on Mike Yorke, Sam Hurst's ramrod. He's a tough huckleberry and likes to burn powder. That's him in the lead. If we have trouble it'll come from Yorke—not Hurst."

The two Sun riders came on without any slackening in pace. They passed the lead cows, flicked rapid glances at their brands, then swung off to block Raines and Ellison.

"What are you doing with those Sun cows?"

demanded Mike Yorke. He was a bluff, coarse-looking individual with a nasal twang in his voice. His cheeks were full and brick-red in color, matching his close-cropped, unruly hair. He was just a bit under six feet, but there was plenty of beef and bone to him. He looked like a hard customer—and was. There was no friendliness in his pale blue eyes.

"Sending them back where they belong, if it's any of your business," Raines told him.

"It sure is my business," snapped Yorke. "The Sun can run its own cows without any help from you."

Raines bristled. "Not when I find them on Chevron grass."

"What do you mean by that?" Sam Hurst cut in.

The Sun owner was thick-shouldered and long of arm. He had a hard, bony face highlighted by slate-gray eyes and a chin that was blunt and square-edged. He was a man well-seasoned by sun and wind. Taciturn by nature, he was, nevertheless, slow to anger.

"I mean," said Raines, his voice honed to a sharp cutting edge, "that somebody cut my line fence up near Wind River and hazed your beef critters through the gap."

"That's a damned lie!" shouted Yorke, his features flaming.

Hurst lifted a hand and said, "They could have drifted through a break in the fence."

Raines's face swelled with wrath. "They didn't drift—they were pushed. And the fence was cut. All three strands in one spot had been snipped off."

Hurst's face showed the faintest hint of surprise as he glanced furtively at his foreman. "You know anything about that, Mike?"

"Hell, no!" rasped Yorke. "If Raines doesn't keep his fences in repair we can't help it if Sun cows slip over the line."

Raines gigged his horse forward, stopping a few feet away from the Sun ramrod. "You're not fooling anybody, Yorke," he said as rage contracted the pupils of his eyes to mere pin points. "We found horse and cattle sign up there around the fence. I figure you hazed those cows over the line yourself, and I'm telling you to keep them on Sun grass unless you want them shot!"

Yorke's big jaw muscles bunched and his hand dropped to the stock of his gun. "You talk mighty big, my friend," he murmured. "Now I'll tell you something. Half of that grass you have under fence doesn't belong to you. It's government land—free graze open to anyone."

"Yeah, but we've been using it for years," said Ellison, speaking for the first time.

"That still doesn't make it yours," growled Yorke.

"Maybe you've got some ideas about taking it over," suggested Raines. There was a grim, toneless quality to his talk.

131

"Maybe I have," snapped Yorke.

Hurst cut in swiftly, "Let it go, Mike."

"What the hell for, Sam?" shouted Yorke. "Raines here has the notion he can build a fence around the whole state of Wyoming and call it his. That Wind River range is open to anybody that needs grass and, by God, if we need it we'll move Sun cows on it."

"You do and you'll buy yourself a range war," warned Raines.

Yorke gave him a nasty grin. He slapped his thigh with the palm of his hand. "Maybe you'd like to settle the matter privately right now—or did you bring your wife along so you could hide behind her skirt?"

Temper boiled over in Raines. He yelled at Melody. "Clear out. Go back to the ranch!" His yellow teeth ground together as he turned back to Yorke. "Damn your soul to hell, we'll smoke this out right now—"

"No!" cried Melody swiftly. Though whatever feeling she had once had for Raines was dead in her, she didn't want to see him shot down. She had seen Mike Yorke shoot a man in the streets of Capricorn—had seen the wicked pleasure crawl in Yorke's eyes when the man dropped with a bullet in his throat. Yorke was a devil with a gun. Violence was like food and drink to him, and he had a tremendous appetite for all three.

Before Raines's hand could drop to the stock of

his .45 Melody was in front of him, clawing at his wrist and slamming him backward.

"Get away!" Raines roared.

But Melody held on, fighting him for possession of the gun. "Stop it, Tom," she pleaded. "Don't be a fool!"

Mike Yorke's brutal laugh cut in. "Your wife is right, Raines. Better take care of your skin."

Raines wrenched away. Melody was thrown to one side. She fell to the ground. She tried to scramble up again. A wild oath ripped from Raines.

"Damn you, Yorke!" he said. "I'll call you!"

The Chevron rancher had completely over-stepped the ropes of caution. He was reckless and uncaring. His right hand hung over his gun like a curved claw.

Yorke grinned in savage anticipation. His right eyelid twitched. Hoot Ellison noted the faint flicker and set himself for the shoot-out. Yorke's hand snapped to his holster, started up again. Then Sam Hurst gigged his horse into Yorke's pony. He cracked a hand against the Sun ramrod's wrist. "That's far enough, Mike!" he said.

Yorke turned, his features black and fierce. "Stay out of this, Sam. Raines is asking for trouble. I'll see he gets it."

Hurst's eyes met Yorke's levelly. He nodded imperceptibly toward Melody, who had now risen and stood anxiously watching the scene. "Let's hang and rattle," he said.

Raines remained in a half-crouch, still not sure of his ground, still not trusting either of the Sun riders.

"What'll it be?" he said.

"We're riding," responded Hurst.

Yorke still looked dark and destructive. He never took kindly to interference. He'd primed himself for killing, and the passion for it was still in him, goading him like a hundred fine needles.

"There'll be another time, Raines," he said. "This thing isn't over and don't you forget it."

Raines watched him without answering. But Hoot Ellison, sitting tense in his saddle just a few feet away from Raines, snapped out his own challenging retort. "We'll be waiting, Mike. Don't make it too long."

Yorke glared at Ellison. "I'll pick the time—and it'll be a time when there are no women around."

The Sun foreman whipped his horse about and trotted after Hurst, who had already started off across the flats.

# Ten

**A** THORNY BUSH slammed into Flood's back as his body plunged downward. It retarded his fall slightly. He made a frantic grab for a root, but it was ripped out of his hand. He bounced off a sharp edge of rock, then rolled face forward into loose shale. It got into his mouth. Dust filmed his throat. He gagged for breath and rolled end over end to the grade's terminus, his shoulders finally jolting against a huge knob of granite.

For a moment he lay stunned and immobile. Then a fit of coughing racked his entire body.

A loud shout far above him woke him to a sense of danger. The dusk had deepened to a deep purple that was almost complete darkness. Muzzle fire bloomed from the cliff top. Bullets spattered the rocks off to his left. Rickard and his men were firing wildly, seeking him out in the uncertain light.

Flood groped for his gun. It was gone. He had lost it in his headlong fall. The roan had trotted away somewhere. He climbed to his feet, feeling a savage ache in all his bones. He felt as if he had been beaten with a rawhide whip.

Above him somebody shouted, "There he is!" and immediately a gun slammed its wicked echo through the hills and a lead slug droned past Flood.

Then Rickard's strident yell rang out. "After him! He can't get away. His horse is gone!"

Immediately a shower of loose stones cascaded down the slope as Rickard led his crew in quick pursuit. Slipping, sliding, half-falling in the loose shale, they came after Flood while the last light in the sky slowly faded into a deep, blue-black band.

Flood stumbled away, angling for a thin line of brush and trees that rimmed the wide ravine. Dust drifted in an invisible screen past him. He heard the wild scramble of his pursuers, and dived into the first tangle of brush he found. It was much thinner than he anticipated. It offered little protection.

"We'll never find him in the dark!" someone grumbled.

"There's the moon," snapped Rickard as the cloud scud that had drawn across the sky suddenly broke away to reveal the round white globe of brilliance high among the stars. "That's all we need."

"Spread out and beat through the brush. If you spot him, pour lead into him. Remember he's Dave Flood, and Calloway wants him dead!"

Silence dropped down upon the ravine—a silence broken only by the sibilant slither of boots on gravel as Rickard's gunmen fanned out in pursuit.

When the moon gaped through the clouds each man was clearly outlined. With a gun he could have potted them easily. There were six of them. He watched them come toward him, guns fisted and the fever of the hunt twisting their faces.

Flood dropped to his hands and knees and groped on through the brush. A grove of trees loomed up and he crawled in that direction. If he stood up, he'd make a clear target for all their guns.

His progress was slow and painful. Behind him came the crunch of leather on gravel, the snapping of twigs. The trees still seemed far away as Flood crawled on.

A sudden glance over his shoulder showed him that one of the renegades was a scant fifty feet away. And the nearest tree was still better than twice that distance from him. Flood sprawled face down in the thicket, partially concealed beneath a thin overhang of branches.

Boots crunched on gravel and loose stones. The steps came steadily on. The bush that hid Flood quivered as the hunter's body rammed into it. A boot slammed into the ground just a few feet away from Flood's face. He lay stiffly quiet, hardly daring to breathe. If he was discovered now, he wouldn't have a chance. He might down this man, but the others would be upon him before he could get away.

The dry dust of the thicket filtered through his nose. It seeped into his throat. The frantic urge to cough racked his lungs. He fought against the impulse, the fierce effort bringing tears to his eyes.

Then the renegade passed on beyond him, and he knew he was safe for the moment. He levered himself back to his hands and knees and peered over his shoulder. The man who had almost trod upon him was now thirty yards away and heading for the thin grove of trees.

A sudden yell ripped through the night. A six-gun cracked once, twice somewhere behind Flood. There was a solid crashing in the trees.

Rickard's voice bellowed a question. "Got him, Jenson?"

Another voice answered immediately. "No, damn it!" Then a horse trotted out of the grove and the voice of the man still hidden in the trees drifted out. "There's Flood's horse!"

Flood saw the big roan gelding he had taken from Calloway swerve toward the foot of the cliff. Then Nap Rickard grabbed the bridle. The spooked horse dragged him a few paces, then stopped.

"Fraley!" Again Rickard's voice boomed out. "Come on over and watch this critter. See that Flood doesn't circle around and grab this roan."

The outlaw came up to Rickard, took the roan's bridle, and led him toward a huge boulder. Rickard moved off to join the rest of his crew.

Flood had to find some way of reaching the roan. And unless he got the roan soon he'd be trapped. For once Rickard took the horse back to Calloway's camp his chance would be gone.

Hidden by the heavy chaparral, Flood kept his attention on the guard. He held the roan's bridle in his left hand, a long-barreled Colt in his right hand. And his eyes never ceased their vigilant scouring of the ravine. But after a little while the guard grew tired of his tedious task and slumped against the boulder at his back.

Then a match flared, and Flood saw the swing of the flame toward the guard's mouth and knew the man had lit a cigarette. Afterward the spent match, still flickering, spiraled through the darkness in a brief, red-yellow arc and sputtered out in the gravel.

Flood's muscles grew cramped. He shifted his position slightly and felt the prick of pain in a dozen places along his bruised body. This slow waiting was more than he could bear. Far off now he could still hear his pursuers shouldering through mesquite and manzanita and scrub brush in their grim search for him.

Rising to a half-crouch, he studied the terrain all around him. A few stunted bushes loomed before him. Beyond that was open ground all the way to the boulder where the horse guard was stationed. With hard gravel underfoot it would be impossible to reach the guard without being heard. Accordingly, Flood decided to run a bluff on the outlaw.

Groping around in the dirt, he found a rock, clamped his fingers around it, and moved out of hiding. As he emerged from the thicket the racket of Rickard's men was becoming louder. That meant they were swinging back to go over the ground they had already covered. It also meant that he hadn't much time to make his break for freedom.

He strode out into the clearing, moving his head from side to side as if he were searching for someone. Out of the corner of his eye he saw the horse guard straighten up and move one pace away from the boulder.

"That you, Jenson?" the guard asked.

"Not a damn sight of Flood," Flood said, keeping his voice muffled.

He moved on toward the guard, who was standing partly in shadow. Flood was clearly limned in the moonlight. He kept his head down, shuffling forward. At any moment he expected the guard to cut loose with an oath and fling up his Colt for a point-blank shot. The air around him grew hot and terribly still. There was menace in it and an awful sense of time running out.

The guard's voice reached him again. "Rickard giving up the hunt?"

"Don't know," Flood retorted gruffly, "but I am."

His fingers tightened around the rock in his fist. A damp, crawling moisture oozed from his skin.

"What the hell are you looking for on the

ground?" demanded the guard as Flood paced nearer.

Flood lifted his head and replied: "Take a guess, friend!"

He dug his boots into the gravel and lunged forward.

"You're not Jenson!" the guard cried, and swung his gun around.

The round black bore of the outlaw's .45 dissolved in a ruddy blob of flame. Flood felt the heat of the powder flare and knew the bullet had missed him by a scant inch. Then his rush carried him against the horse guard, and smashed the rock against the side of the renegade's jaw. The outlaw's eyes rolled crazily in his head and he pitched forward on his face.

Flood stepped aside as the guard fell, then bent down to get the gun that had slipped from his fingers. In the next instant he had moved to the roan and heaved himself up into the saddle.

A shout from the woods told him that Rickard's men had heard the guard's shot and were coming to investigate. Flood galloped off in the opposite direction. He had traveled only fifty yards when he saw that the ravine came to an abrupt end at a perpendicular wall of rock. The only way out was back the way he had come—which meant he'd have to ride through a gantlet of hot lead with Rickard and his crowd on the firing end.

Even as he whirled the roan around for the dash

back down the ravine, Flood saw one man emerge from a thicket. Flood raked the roan with his spurs. The animal lunged forward in a fast run.

The renegade called out, "Who is that?" Then he noticed the guard's limp body sprawled near the boulder and yelled a quick warning to the others. "Watch out! Flood's loose. He's got his horse!"

An answering shout issued from the grove of trees where Rickard had vanished. Flood drove the roan straight toward the man who had sounded the warning. The outlaw wheeled around. Muzzle light whipped from his drawn gun. A brace of slugs winged past Flood, narrowly missing him. Then he swung his own .45 across his body and slammed two fast shots at the running outlaw. Suddenly the man stumbled, whirled around, and went down.

At the same instant Nap Rickard burst out into the clearing, his gun yammering. A bullet slammed into Flood's saddle skirt, tearing a wide furrow in the leather. Flood returned the shot, but the roan's bucking motion jarred his aim. Seconds later he was past Rickard and racing into the grove with Rickard's gun emptying its load of lead at him.

Other men were crashing through the brush, angling toward the scene. But only one of them got within shooting distance. The fellow wasted three snap shots that went wide of the mark. Then Flood was clear and clattering down the ravine.

# Eleven

SHERIFF SYD STACK was sprawled in a battered barrel chair with his booted feet propped up on a paper-littered desk when Dave Flood came through the open doorway. Stack threw down the stockman's journal he had been reading and leaped to his feet. A walnut-handled Colt jutted from his fist when he straightened up.

"Flood, you're a fool for coming back here to Blue Mesa," he said. "Put up your hands."

Flood paused in the doorway. A tight grin stirred his upper lip. He slid the heavy saddlebags off his shoulder and moved toward the lawman's desk.

"Stay where you are," Stack warned.

"You won't need your gun, Sheriff," Flood told him.

The lawman's Colt didn't deviate a fraction of an inch in its line-up on Flood's chest. Flood stopped. With a swing of his body he threw the saddlebags on Stack's desk. The movement sent the sheriff lurching to one side. His eyes narrowed, and for a moment Flood thought he was going to squeeze off a shot.

"Turn around and face the door," ordered Stack.

Flood stared levelly at the sheriff. Stack looked back at him, grim and unsmiling. Flood turned slowly and lifted his hands. He heard Stack move around the desk and come up behind him. There was a faint pressure in his holster, then a sudden lightness as Stack took charge of his gun.

"All right," said Stack. As Flood turned, the sheriff added: "I suppose you realize you're under arrest."

Faint lines bracketed Flood's mouth corners. He said, "Take a look inside those saddlebags and you may change your ideas about putting me under arrest."

"What's your game, Flood?" Stack demanded suspiciously.

Flood gestured to the leather pouches on the lawman's desk. "Remember the money that was stolen from the Blue Mesa bank a few days ago? You'll find it inside those bags."

The thin surface of Stack's lips pressed together. His leathery skin drew tight around the thin bones of his face. The guarded, skeptical look never left his eyes.

Finally he retreated to the desk. Keeping his attention partly on Flood and partly on the saddlebags, he sent his left hand exploring the depths of the pouches. He drew out several cloth bags, opened them, and dumped out bundles of currency.

"If you have someone from the bank count the bills, I think you'll find it's all there," Flood told him.

The sheriff looked up from the desk. His weather-wrinkled eyes were cloudy with puzzlement.

"So you decided to double-cross your friends," he said at last.

"They were no friends of mine," Flood snapped. "I had no part in that bank holdup. But with the crowd feeling the way it did about things I figured it was better to make a run for it. After all, a man can't do much to help himself while he's sitting in a jail cell."

Stack's angular body craned forward. He said, dry-voiced: "I reckon it's time you did some talking about this." He pointed to the packets of money scattered on the desk.

"That's what I'm here for," Flood replied. "I left Blue Mesa in a considerable hurry the other day for two reasons. One was to save my neck. The other was to get that bank money and bring it back—because I could think of no other way to clear myself."

Flood stopped, watching Stack to note his reaction. The sheriff's features remained non-committal. "Get on with it," he said gruffly.

Rapidly Flood reviewed his activities after fleeing from Blue Mesa. He told of his long search through the Tetons before stumbling upon the outlaw camp. And he told also of the gunfight with Calloway and Trotter and the subsequent encounter in the ravine with Rickard's men.

However, to protect himself, Flood used false names in referring to the three renegades. He reasoned that if Stack had any old reward posters lying around the mention of the real names of Calloway or Trotter would immediately link him with the others.

When Flood had finished Stack said quietly, "You say you killed one of the outlaws? What about the other fellow you shot?"

"He was badly hurt. I put two bullets in him."

Stack regarded Flood carefully. "How did you know where to look for those men?"

"The Tetons are the only place to hide in this country. I don't have to tell you that. The rest was luck."

"I'm thinking of Nell Raines," said the sheriff, "and of how she said she saw you talking to those three jiggers outside the saloon. What's your explanation of that?"

Flood gave the lawman an irritated glance. "I'd met them before in Arizona, but they weren't friends. In fact, I had a run-in with one of them in a poker game in Phoenix. Caught him dealing off the bottom of the deck. When I called him on it he tried to burn me down. I beat him to the shot and nicked his arm. He swore he'd get me for that."

"Still, he didn't come shooting when he saw you the other day."

A red tide of color washed over Flood's cheeks.

His voice was rough and thin-edged when he replied. "That surprised me too. He was mighty friendly. It made me suspicious. I know now that he saw me come in with the Chevron trail herd and figured I'd be collecting the money for the cows. That's how the three of them got the idea of holding me up in the hotel. And it was just blind chance that I happened to pass the bank the next morning as they were ready to make their getaway. As I told you then, I tried to put a hitch in their plans. But they saw a chance to frame me into a hang noose by pretending I was with them."

The sheriff's seamed features relaxed a trifle. He let the barrel of his gun slant away from Flood's chest. "And what about the Chevron trail herd money?" he asked.

Flood tapped his lean waist. "It's all right here in a money belt—every cent of it. The Chevron is my next stop."

Stack watched Flood, studying him with a careful intentness. There was no mistaking the toughness in Flood, the hard purpose in his level eyes. And there was no mistaking the fact that he had driven himself to the limit of his endurance during the past few days. Weariness had left its mark in the shadow pools under his eyes and in the gaunt lines of his face on which several purplish bruises showed.

The sheriff suddenly thrust Flood's gun toward

him. Flood took the weapon, thrust it back into his holster, and gave Stack a quizzical glance.

"I may be wrong," said Stack, "but I think you're telling it straight. The fact that you've returned the stolen bank money proves that as far as I'm concerned."

"Thanks."

"Don't thank me, Flood. You've earned the right to have your story believed. You may have trouble with Tom Raines."

"I'm expecting it," Flood told him. He started toward the door, then paused and looked back. "Was there anything else on your mind?"

"That's all," said Stack. "I may take a run into the Tetons and have a look around for that outlaw bunch. If I do, I may want you to tag along."

"It'll probably be a waste of time. They wouldn't be likely to hang around in the hills after what happened."

"Unless," said Stack, "they had some idea of getting back at you."

Flood considered the sheriff's idea, then shrugged it off. He nodded to Stack and went out, going immediately to his horse.

The following afternoon Flood rode up to the headquarters buildings of the Chevron ranch. Two punchers, working in the breaking corral, glanced through the screen of dust kicked up by a pair of steel-gray broncs and immediately ducked through the bars and came running toward him.

Tightness grew in Flood's shoulder blades as he wondered what kind of reception he would receive. The puncher in the lead was Whip Anders, young and blond-haired and quick-tempered. The other was Ray Allbright, a new hand and pretty much of an unknown quantity.

Flood got as far as the edge of the veranda when Anders and his partner reached the foot of the steps leading up to the front door of the ranch house.

"This is as far as you go, Flood," said Anders. He flipped his Colt out. His thin, strained face was twisted in a grimace of dislike. The change startled Flood, for he had always liked the young puncher. Now he saw how things would be here. Every man would be braced against him.

"Take it easy, Whip," Flood murmured. "I want to see Raines."

"You'll see him at the end of a gun barrel."

The front door flew open and banged against the wall. Tom Raines charged out on the veranda. His harsh voice slammed at Flood like a closed fist. "Get down off your horse, Flood. You won't be riding again."

Flood climbed down, his hands kept well away from his gun belt. His eyes were level and cool, but there were tiny beads of moisture on his long upper lip. A killing lust surged through Raines. It choked his face with blood, made the veins in his throat stand out like thick cables.

"I've got something for you, Tom," Flood told him.

"Shut up!" growled Raines thickly. "You've got no friends here. I don't know what brought you to the Chevron, but you can take my oath that this is the end of the line for you."

Raines started down the veranda steps. His heavy tread bowed each plank. He reached the bottom as Flood's hands lifted to his belt. Raines's voice slashed at him immediately. "Move your hand another inch and I'll blast your belt buckle right through your guts." Raines snapped a command to Anders. "Whip, get his gun."

The puncher circled behind Flood. He moved warily, his gun lifted and ready for instant use. Flood stood still, his features dark and outwardly composed. But inside the pressure was like a giant vise squeezing all the nerve fibers of his body. Anders came up close, grabbed his gun, and slid quickly out of range.

"I've got it, Tom," Anders said.

As he spoke the puncher's gaze lifted to the veranda. Flood followed the direction of his glance and saw that Melody and Nell, attracted by the commotion in the yard, had come out of the house.

Melody gave him a smile, her eyes suddenly bright and eager. Except for a brief expression of startled surprise, Nell showed no emotion.

Flood's mouth tightened. The pupils of his eyes contracted. He realized he hadn't expected anything else from Nell, yet her coldness left him with an unutterable feeling of loss.

"Dave, I knew you'd come back," Melody told him. "Are you all right?"

Raines whirled on her. "Damn it, Melody, this is the man who stole my trail herd money and you've got the gall to welcome him back. Get inside and stay out of this."

But Melody stayed where she was, her willowy, high-breasted figure taut with fear when she noted Raines's angry red-rimmed eyes.

Raines turned back to Flood. He kept his gun trained on the battered nickel buckle of Flood's gun belt. His thick lips moved to speak, but Anders's sharp tones broke in upon him. "What'll we do with him?"

It was Flood who answered. "Before you answer that, Tom, you might be interested in the money belt strapped under my shirt."

Raines's brows drew together. He squinted up at Flood. "What money belt?"

"The one containing the Chevron trail herd money."

Up on the veranda Melody gasped in surprise. But no one paid any attention to her. Raines's reaction was one of swift rage. "Damn you, Flood, I'll take no hoorawing about that money. You stole it and I'll have your hide for it."

Flood's eyes chilled. His voice laid a sudden hot challenge across the dust to Raines. "Shoot any damn time you please, but the money is in this belt." Quickly Flood's hands fumbled underneath his shirt. He opened the lower button, pulled one end of the shirt free, then unstrapped the wide leather belt hidden beneath it. He held it out to Raines, and when the latter still refused to make a motion toward it, he tossed it at the rancher's feet.

Anders darted forward and picked up the belt. He opened up the thick, wadded pouch, then stopped, his face registering shocked unbelief when he saw the currency stacked inside.

"Let me have that!" growled Raines. Anders passed the belt to the rancher.

"You don't have to count it," said Flood. "It's all there."

There was a flutter of footsteps along the veranda and down the crude plank stairs. Melody rushed up beside Raines to look at the belt. "I knew it, Tom," she said. "I knew Dave would be back with the money."

"Thanks, Melody," Flood murmured stiffly. "I'm glad somebody believed that."

He looked toward Nell, now at the head of the steps. She blushed, and her warm red mouth looked suddenly crushed and beaten.

Raines's anger drained completely away. An

agony of doubt and bewilderment filled him. "How did you get it?" he asked gruffly.

Flood told him, repeating the same story he had given Sheriff Stack in Blue Mesa.

"Why did you ever take such terrible chances?" Melody demanded. "You should have gotten help."

"Where would I have gotten it?" Flood asked her. "Here at the Chevron, or in Blue Mesa?"

Melody's features flattened. She nodded. "You're right. There was no help to be had."

Raines thrust her aside impatiently. "All right, Melody. You've had your say." Then he looked at Flood in obvious discomfort. "I don't know what to say. I had it pegged wrong. You took one hell of a chance."

"I didn't see any other way. I had to bring that money back or never show my face in this country again."

Raines said thickly, "There's not much I can say except thanks."

"That's enough," Flood told him. He glanced toward Nell, saw her eyes intent upon him. He said, "You still figure those fellows in Blue Mesa were friends of mine?"

"I—I was wrong, Dave," Nell told him. Her voice was faint and her eyes were stricken. There was a strange set to her soft mouth.

Flood waited for her to go on. But she said nothing more and she turned her face away when

Melody and the others swung toward her. He knew then that something had gone out of their relationship, something he couldn't reclaim. It puzzled him and at the same time it drained him of all emotion except wounded pride.

Raines and Anders and Allbright stood rooted in the yard. None of them said anything. He couldn't understand their silence. There was a quality of strain about it that was unnatural. He felt shut out.

"I'll take my gun, Anders," he said.

Anders handed it over without question. Flood thrust it into his holster and stepped to his horse. They watched him mount, and still no one spoke, and the feeling of constraint in the yard grew more and more unbearable. He kicked the roan into motion and drifted out of the yard.

At every step the roan took he expected to hear Nell or Melody or Raines call him back. But the roan cantered across the yard, cut into the Chevron private road that led to the main road to town without anyone breaking the silence.

Flood knew then that he still hadn't gained Raines's trust. He'd risked his neck on a dangerous long-shot gamble to get Raines's money and now he could ride out and never come back. And Nell . . . The thought of her and the bleak emptiness that lay between them jabbed at him like the cutting edge of a knife. There was the dry, bitter taste of ashes in his mouth. He dug his heels into the roan's flanks. The animal answered the prod with a burst of speed. The sun was hot and the wind was hot. They seared his skin. But the pain was good and clean—not like that other burning pain deep inside him.

# Twelve

MELODY RAINES was the first one to speak after Flood rode away. "I hope you're proud of yourself," she said sharply to Nell. "You've regarded Dave as an outlaw all along. Now that he's proved he was on the level the only thing you can say is that you were wrong. Not another word. Not a word to tell him you're sorry."

"I—I couldn't say anything else just then," Nell murmured. Her face was a ruddy crimson and the words issued from her slowly, as if the act of talking had become an intolerable effort. "I thought of the terrible risks he must have taken, but I was too choked up inside to tell him how I felt."

Scorn flattened Melody's lips into a thin crease. "That's a fine answer. What you probably mean is that you were too proud to admit how much you wronged him."

Raines took Melody's arm, swung her around to him. "Seems to me you're mighty concerned about Flood," he said.

"It's about time you became concerned yourself," Melody retorted. She pushed Raines's hand away from her arm. "I hate to see a man get a raw deal. And that's just what Dave is getting from you and all of us here. Everybody on the Chevron as well as in town has been calling him a thief and a renegade—a man who violated your trust. Then you learn that he hasn't double-crossed you or robbed you after all. Instead, he's taken his life into his hands and run risks even you yourself wouldn't take in order to get back the money that was stolen. And he did it without help. Did you forget that he left Blue Mesa with a posse on his heels? Did you forget that you'd ordered the Chevron hands to shoot him on sight? And can you guess the kind of odds he faced going into the Tetons after three tough outlaws while two trigger-happy posses were combing the country looking for him?"

Melody paused, her breathing very rapid, her face flushed with emotion. Then she continued heatedly. "Dave did that for you and the Chevron. The odds were ten to one he'd never pull the game out. But he came through and he brought back the money. And what do you do?" Again Melody stopped, her upper lip twisted in a gesture of contempt. "You say thanks and let him ride out of here as if he were a broken-down cowpuncher riding what you people call the grub line."

Raines scowled in discomfort. He rubbed the palm of one hand against the gray-black stubble of his beard. "What can I do?" he asked.

"You know the answer to that," Melody told him. "You'll never find a better ramrod than Dave Flood. Offer him his job back."

"He'd never take it after the way I treated him."

"How do you know if you don't ask him?"

Nell came slowly down the steps and joined them. "Melody's right, Tom," she said. "We're all to blame for what's happened. But most of it falls on my head. I started things off in Blue Mesa by insisting that Dave must be friends of the three men who held up the bank. I refused to believe him when he said he tried to stop the holdup. My insistence that Dave was lying helped turn Sheriff Stack and everyone else in Blue Mesa against him. It's up to me to make amends. I'll ride after him and bring him back."

She started to walk around Melody, but the other girl restrained her. "Never mind," said Melody. "You had your chance there on the veranda when he asked you if you still thought those three renegades were friends of his. You held back. If anyone goes after him it'll be me."

Raines cut in strongly. "You'll stay here, Melody." She glared at him and he added, "It's not your place to go. Nell or I should go."

"Let me go, Tom," said Nell. "I'll never forgive myself if I don't."

"I reckon I ought to go with you," Raines said ruefully.

"It'll be all right. I know you were planning to go up to Wind River with Whip Anders. I'll tell Dave. I'll make him understand."

Melody's eyes clouded with displeasure. She

said stiffly, "Go ahead. I'd laugh if he refused to talk to you."

"That'll be enough, Melody," said Raines.

There was derision in the glance she gave her husband. But she moved back up the steps as Nell hurried off to the corral. Whip Anders preceded Nell, ducking through the bars to rope out a horse for her.

Melody lingered on the veranda while Anders saddled a bay mare for Nell and then threw rigs on two other horses for Raines and himself. Nell cantered out of the yard, heading for Capricorn, while Raines and Anders struck north toward the Wind River line camp.

The derisive smile remained constant on Melody's lips as she held her station on the veranda. When Nell rode out of sight over the brow of a low hill Melody suddenly called out to the puncher who had remained behind at the ranch.

"Ray, saddle up that pinto of mine. I'm going riding."

Allbright's answer carried back to her from the corral. "Sure thing, Mrs. Raines."

She came down the veranda steps and hurried across the yard. She stood impatiently by the corral all the while the puncher rigged the blanket and saddle on her horse. When he gave her a hand up to the saddle she didn't even thank him. She whirled the animal around and went galloping past the ranch house in the direction of town.

For the first mile or so Melody followed the main wagon road that wandered by devious curves into Capricorn. Then, reaching a narrow trail that lifted over a high, brushy hogback, she reined the pinto off the road. The trail was a seldom-used short cut into town. She'd ridden it once or twice before with Raines. Though it was rough going and hazardous in one area where it threaded the lip of a high gorge, she took it because she was intent upon reaching Capricorn ahead of Nell.

A man on a good horse could save twenty minutes on the trip to town by using the short cut. In Melody's case she gained only ten minutes. Even then she might not have saved any time at all if Nell, traveling the main road, hadn't followed a rather leisurely pace.

Melody rode straight to Capricorn's only hotel, a two-story weathered frame building wedged between a hay-and-feed barn on one side and a saloon on the other. Several saddle horses were tethered to the hitch rack in front of the hotel, but the lobby was empty of visitors when she entered and hurried up to the desk.

The hollow-eyed clerk rose from a splintered barrel chair. His yellow-toothed mouth spread in a wide grin. "What can I do for you, Mrs. Raines?" he inquired.

"I'm looking for Dave Flood," she said rather

breathlessly. "Has he been in here this afternoon?"

The clerk peered closely at her, his eyes shrewd and knowing. He said, "Yeah. Just rented him a room about twenty minutes ago. Shall I go up and tell him you want to see him?"

He started around the plain board counter. Melody's quick voice stopped him. "Never mind. I'll see him myself. Just tell me the number of his room."

The shrewd eyes bored into Melody, and she felt heat gather in her cheeks. But the clerk bent to the register in front of him. When he looked up his face was bland. "Room twelve at the end of the hall upstairs," he told her.

Without bothering to thank him, Melody moved to the stairs and mounted to the second floor. She hurried down the dimly lit corridor until she reached room twelve. For a moment she hesitated outside the door, listening for some sounds of occupancy. She heard a board squeak, then heard the splash of water in a basin. Quickly she knocked.

"Come on in," Flood's voice directed her.

The knob turned in Melody's hand and she pushed the door inward. Flood was crouched over a basin of soapy water. He had just finished shaving the dark beard stubble off his chin. He was bare to the waist. Involuntarily her eyes slid from his face to his broad, powerful chest, crisscrossed with ropelike muscles, then down to his flat stomach. She watched the play of his shoulder and arm muscles as he swung around from the cracked, flyspecked mirror nailed to the wall above the basin.

"Dave," she murmured, moving farther into the room, "I've come to bring you back to the Chevron."

Flood picked up a towel from the battered dresser and slowly dried his face. He said, "Did Tom send you?"

"Yes," Melody told him.

"Why didn't he come himself?"

Melody smiled, her eyes nagging at him like a soft, groping hand. "I asked him to let me go," she said. "Please, Dave. You've been terribly wronged. Tom realizes that. But he was afraid that after what happened—with him thinking the way he did—you wouldn't want to work for him again."

Flood's fingers tightened around the towel, bunching it into a fluffy soiled white ball. "Maybe he's right, Melody," he said out of the dark bitterness that filled him.

She rushed forward, her features frozen in quick concern. "No, Dave. Don't feel that way." She halted within a few inches of him.

He looked down at her, grim and unsmiling. "Are you sure this isn't just your own idea?" he asked.

Melody moved close to him—so close that her body brushed lightly against him. Her long-fingered hands gripped his arms. "Please—Dave, you've got to—to believe me." There was a catch in her voice as if it had jammed in her throat. "We all want you back."

"All?" It was just the one word, terse and blunt.

Melody knew he was thinking about Nell. Did she want him back too? That's what he was asking her. But when he looked down into Melody's jade-green eyes he saw no answer to his unspoken question. He saw, instead, a warm and heady darkness—a darkness that had a strange magnetic pull, drawing him down into a bottomless well. Sudden fire flashed its way along his taut nerves, leaving them dully aching. He tried to lock his mind against Melody. He dropped the towel. It slid silently to the bare puncheon floor. Afterward he knotted his hands into fists. It was the only way he could keep from grabbing her.

He told himself that this wild, savage rush of feeling was all wrong. He didn't love Melody. It was Nell he wanted. Yet when Melody stood so near to him, with all of her womanly charms so bright before him and the hot hunger in her eyes so clearly shining, it took all the force of his will to refrain from touching her.

"Yes, all of us," Melody finally told him, and her caressing glance slid from his face down to his chest again, to the great muscular spread of it, to the thin mat of brown hair that covered it. Then she added in a whisper: "But, most of all, *I* want you back!"

There was a strange dark stirring in Flood's bruised face. He drew a long, ragged breath. Suddenly Melody came full against him. He felt the warm thrust of her pointed breasts against his chest. Then her hands reached up and pulled his head down. Roughly she brought his mouth against hers.

Flood's restraint snapped. He hooked his arms around Melody. Her lips slid away from his mouth and she moaned, "My darling," as the hard, lean length of him responded to the straining pressure of her body.

Then her mouth came back to his, warm and open and eager. Back and forth, back and forth her lips smashed and ground against his. He felt her hot breath in his throat. She was like a tigress. Her hands clawed the back of his neck. Her lips were a lush trap from which there was no escape—and in that whirling moment Flood didn't want to escape.

They were still standing there, locked in each other's arms, all their rash and violent compulsions swaying them, when they heard the protesting squeak of the door hinges behind them. Flood pulled roughly away, his breathing heavy and uneven.

"Sorry," said Nell coldly from the open doorway. "I didn't mean to interrupt."

"Nell!" The word broke from Flood in a hoarse shout. He saw how her deep blue eyes turned dark with anger, and her lips were pressed tightly together with tiny white arcs of strain at their corners. "I—I'm glad you came," he said lamely.

Her eyes were like a white-hot flame touching him briefly, then moving to Melody. "I see I'm a little late," she said.

Melody straightened her hair, tucked her yellow shirt more firmly into her divided skirt. Her mouth crinkled in faint amusement. "Yes, I've already invited Dave back to the Chevron."

"And you've had his answer."

The quiet hardness in Nell's statement shook Dave. He wanted to tell her how sorry he was that she had found Melody in his arms. He was a plain damned fool. Finding them in each other's arms must have hit her like a slap in the face. But he understood the fierce pride in Nell and he knew there was nothing he could say to make amends. He felt shamed and miserable.

While he groped frantically for some words to cover the embarrassed silence that had fallen upon them, Nell said, "I came to make my apologies. I wronged you by saying and believing the things I did." The words were spoken mechanically, as if she had memorized them. There was no feeling, no expression behind them. But inside her heart was fiercely crying: *I hate you, I hate you! Why did you make me love you? Even now I want your arms around me and your mouth against mine. Yet I despise you for kissing Melody. You've done it before and you'll do it again—because she's the kind of woman she is and she wants you at any price!*

The tension in Flood eased. He said eagerly, "It's all right, Nell. I don't blame you. I can see how it must have looked."

He started forward, his hand outstretched. But her eyes were suddenly misty with tears, and she turned away from him and hurried into the hall.

Flood ran after her. "Nell, wait!" he called.

But she continued down the dimly lit corridor, heading for the stairs. He watched her disappear. Then Melody came out to him, took him by the arm.

"Let her go, Dave. What do you care?"

He looked at her levelly. All the passion was gone out of him. The invitation in her jade-green eyes went unheeded. "I reckon you'd better go, too, Melody," he said.

"But, Dave—" she started to protest.

"Let me alone," he said, more roughly this time.

"But you—you're coming back to the ranch?"

"I'm coming back," he said, "but not until later."

Something in his eyes warned Melody not to press him any further. She gave him a smile that was not returned, then walked past him down the hotel corridor.

# Thirteen

**B**ILL CALLOWAY was still clinging to consciousness when Nap Rickard and his followers clambered back up the steep slope and returned to the outlaw camp. Sprawled on the ground, his breathing thin and shallow, the blood on his shirt making a dark stain in the feeble flames of the dying fire, Calloway rasped a hoarse question at Rickard. "Did you get Flood?"

"No. He got away." Rickard, weary and out of breath from his climb, crouched beside Calloway. "You hit bad?" he inquired.

"Never mind about me," snapped Calloway, his feverish eyes raking the hard-visaged renegades grouped behind Rickard. "How did you fools let him get away?"

Rickard cursed luridly for a second or two. Then he said, "We had him pretty well penned up in the brush. One of the boys caught his roan and I left a guard with the critter. But Flood circled around us, jumped the guard, and got his horse. He rode right through us."

"Damn you, Rickard!" growled Calloway, trying to lurch up on one elbow, then sinking back to the ground with a gruff gasp of pain. "There were six of you and you let him get away. I—I ought to gut-shoot you—the whole damned lot of you. That wasn't Flood's horse. It was mine, and every cent of that bank money as well as the Chevron trail herd money was in the saddlebags that critter was carrying."

Calloway's fierce outburst left him gagging for breath. Fresh blood welled out of the wound high in his chest. His eyes flickered closed. Then they opened again, and he glared at Rickard.

Rickard's sharp, narrow-angled jaw jutted forward as he bent close to Calloway. "Speaking of odds, Bill, you didn't do so well. You're packing two hunks of lead and I see Ed Trotter lying dead yonder."

Calloway's eyes dilated. He tried to speak but choked on the words. One of the men behind Rickard said, "Nap, you'd better do something about that hole in his chest. That blood is leaking out fast."

Rickard nodded and bent quickly to Calloway. He ripped away the upper section of the outlaw leader's shirt, revealing the raw, ugly lips of the bullet wound. "Heap some more wood on that fire," he said to the man nearest to him. When the man moved off to obey he directed another man to get some water heated in a pan.

Calloway sank into unconsciousness while Rickard went on with his preparations. He tore a strip of cloth from his undershirt and wadded it temporarily against the wound. Then he rolled up Calloway's trouser leg, trying to get at his thigh wound. The levis Calloway was wearing, however, fitted too snugly to permit them to be rolled all the way up. Rickard finally had to loosen Calloway's belt and slip his levis down over his hips.

He was still fumbling with the thigh wound when the outlaw who had been directed to get some hot water approached him with a steaming pan. "How does he look?" the man asked.

Rickard shook his head. "I don't like that chest wound. We're going to have to get him to a doctor as fast as we can. The best thing I can do for him now is to clean the wounds and stop the bleeding."

With more strips torn from his undershirt Rickard cleaned away the dirt and blood from the lips of the chest wound. Then he quickly wadded more cloth against the hole and secured it with some thin twine wound twice around Calloway's body. He made a similar bandage for the wound in Calloway's thigh. When he had finished he noticed that Calloway's eyes were open. Agony was mirrored in the muddy depths of those eyes, but he managed to talk.

"Thanks—Nap—for fixing me up," he murmured.

Hunkered closely beside Calloway with the flames of the nearby campfire giving his cheeks an unnatural ruddy hue, Rickard said, "You're not out of the woods yet, Bill. The slug that hit your leg went right on through without hitting any bone as far as I can see. But you're still packing lead in your chest. That's what worries me. I've stopped the bleeding, but you're going to need a doctor. It'll be a rough trip taking you into Capricorn, but I don't see any other way out of it."

"Not Capricorn," Calloway murmured. "It's too dangerous."

Rickard nodded. His weathered features pulled into a line of strict and savage concentration. "Damn it! What can we do?" He thought a moment longer, then said, "The only other thing is for me to go into Capricorn and bring a sawbones out with me—by gunpoint if necessary." He rose from his crouched position, hitched up his gun belt.

Calloway's right arm lifted in a feeble, restraining gesture. "Wait, Nap!" he said hoarsely. "You know that—little—trail fork town across the Tetons called Benton?"

"Hell, that's too damned far."

Calloway shook his head slowly. Pain still glazed his eyes, and it was a distinct effort for him to talk. "I—I'll have to chance it," he said. "Get me—there." He paused, his throat muscles moving sluggishly. His tongue, thick with approaching fever, crept out to moisten his dry lips. "Couple miles this side of Benton—there's a—small cattle outfit run by—by Jack Fargo.

171

See—him." The words were coming more slowly now, as if Calloway were dragging them up through his windpipe one by one. "Get—me—there—he'll—know—what—to—do."

.

# Fourteen

BACK at the Chevron, Flood found things fitting themselves into the old established routine. At first Raines felt a little awkward with Flood and showed it by avoiding him for a few days. The rancher had made his apologies in his customary blunt fashion. And Flood, sensing the sincerity in Raines's manner, made light of what had happened.

Soon he was deeply involved in the regular round of ranching chores—checking the condition of various beef herds scattered over the range, moving one herd from grazed-out land to fresh pasture, supervising rotted and broken-down sections of line fence, and taking four days to ride over to Laramie to arrange for the purchase of two blooded bulls for breeding purposes.

The range work kept Flood away from headquarters much of the time. Consequently he saw little of Nell or Melody. Melody sought opportunities to be with him. In fact, on two occasions he met her high in the hills where she had gone for a "ride." Nell, too, went for rides, but she seemed to avoid the areas of Chevron range where Flood was working.

Several times Flood tried to engage her in conversation, but she always managed to put him off with some excuse. Once he caught her at the corral as she was waiting for one of the hands to saddle up a mare for her to ride. However, Raines came along from the barn at the same time and called Flood aside to discuss the matter of buying a few more cutting horses for use in the fall roundup. As Flood turned away to join Raines he saw the quick look of relief that passed over Nell's features.

Several weeks later they met unexpectedly on the road to town. Nell had gone to Capricorn early in the day to see a seamstress friend about a fitting for a dress. Flood was on his way in to town to leave an order with the harness maker for some new wagon harness. They came face to face around a sharp bend in the road. Flood started to rein up and said, "Howdy, Nell."

She answered unsmilingly, "Hello," and kept going, meaning to pass close to his left.

A sudden impulse made Flood swing his roan gelding across the road in front of the girl. He caught the bridle of her chestnut mare.

"Nell," he said, "we don't see much of each other."

She glanced briefly at him, then stared beyond him. "I've been busy and so have you," she murmured.

"Not that busy," he said.

Nell shrugged and fiddled impatiently with the reins. Her heart was pounding like a triphammer beneath her ribs. Of all the men she had known there was no man who affected her as deeply as Dave Flood. Just to be near him filled her with a strange sweet weakness. But it was a weakness she now despised in herself, and so she locked her lips against him, and the glance she showed him held the gray and cold blankness of a stone wall.

Desperate with his need for her, Flood tried again. "Nell, what's the matter between us?"

She kept her back stiff and her voice was brutally careful when she answered him. "Is there something wrong?"

Flood's hand tightened on the chestnut mare's reins. The magic of Nell's nearness turned him and caught all his desires until nothing else mattered except his aching want for her.

"You've been avoiding me, Nell," he said roughly. "If it's Melody you're worried about—"

She cut in icily, "I didn't mention her name."

"You don't have to. I can see you're remembering that afternoon in the hotel in town."

"I'm remembering nothing." Nell's eyes gave him nothing. And her clipped, terse speech gave him nothing.

The roan gelding shifted closer to the mare. Flood leaned forward. Every muscle in his face was drawn with strain. "Forget Melody," he said. "She means nothing to me."

A deep, long-drawn breath ran out of Nell. Dark blue smudges lined her eyes. She said, "I'm not interested one way or the other."

One of Flood's cheek muscles began to twitch. The inside of his mouth felt dry and bruised. A tortured desperation ripped away all his restraint. "You're wrong, Nell—so wrong." Suddenly he reached out and pulled her into the hard circle of his arms. She fought him for a moment, averting her face from his seeking mouth. Then she went limp, and he forced his lips down on hers with almost ruthless force.

Passion churned along every quivering nerve. His arms were a crushing weight and his greedy mouth couldn't get enough of her. But in a moment Flood knew it was hopeless. Her lips lay still and cool and unresisting beneath his. She let him have his way with her mouth, but now there was no life, no spark in her. All the magic that was in her was gone. Suddenly Flood felt chilled and lost.

He dropped his arms and leaned back in the saddle. Nell drew away from him. Carefully and deliberately she scrubbed the back of her hand across the scarlet curve of her mouth.

"Are you quite sure you've finished?" she asked. There wasn't any anger in her voice—just a vacant deadness. But it tore at Flood's emotions like no degree of rage could ever have done.

"Forgive me, Nell," he begged.

"There's nothing to forgive," she said crisply. "Just leave me alone."

Loneliness swirled all around Flood. The angles of his cheekbones turned sharp. "Is that the way you want it?"

"Yes," she answered. "That's the way I want it." She retrieved the mare's reins. She looked at him without seeing him. "Am I free to go now?"

The cold politeness of the question drove Flood back. He swung the roan halfway across the road. "Go ahead, Nell. I'll not stand in your way."

She slapped the mare into a trot and rode on without another glance. And Flood stayed rooted to his saddle, watching her grow smaller and smaller in the distance until he lost her in the haze of dust stirred into motion by the mare's hoofs.

It was later the same day, as Flood was cantering into the Chevron ranch yard after returning from Capricorn, that the first event in a new chain of trouble took place. It was a preview of other greater tumult to come. But at the time there was no reason for Flood to be particularly alarmed—the alarm was to come later.

A rider slouched in the saddle of a rawboned black gelding, talking to Nell who stood at the top of the veranda steps. Flood pushed on a little faster, idly wondering who the visitor was. Even when he recognized Mike Yorke, ramrod of the Sun outfit, he was not perturbed.

He drifted up to the visiting foreman. He had

never particularly liked Yorke. The man's truculence and aggressiveness did not invite friendship. But now range courtesy dictated Flood's greeting. "Hello, Mike. Climb down and rest your legs."

"I'll stay where I am," said Yorke.

Flood looked inquiringly at Nell. She told him, "Yorke says someone set fire to one of Sun ranch's big grazing meadows. He seems to think you might know something about it." With that Nell turned around and went inside the house.

"You came to the wrong place, Mike," Flood said.

Yorke's heavily browned face held a deep-seated weariness. His hands were black with soot and there were streaks of it on his cheeks and along his forehead. "I'm not so sure of that, Flood."

Flood felt the unhinging swing of temper, but he kept his voice level and controlled. "I reckon you'd better explain that, Mike."

"That's what I'm here for," snapped Yorke. He was in an ugly mood and keyed to violence.

In sharp nasal tones he told of coming upon the meadow with a couple other Sun riders and finding it fully ablaze along a half-mile line. They'd had a two-hour battle to bring the fire under control. By that time most of the grass in the pasture had been burned to a crisp. A careful survey of the area had revealed the sign of several horses and numbers of burnt matches in a half-dozen widely scattered spots.

"That was a set fire, Flood," he concluded.

"It sure sounds that way."

"What I want to know is where you and the Chevron hands were today," Yorke demanded.

Flood's thoughts were abruptly keen-edged and vivid. "Don't go too far, Mike," he said. "I'm not explaining my actions to you or anyone else. And while you're here you can give your reasons for labeling the Chevron with the blame."

"It's simple enough," growled Yorke. "We followed that hoof sign we found and it led toward the Chevron."

"That's interesting," said Flood quietly, though his face was grim. "And you followed the sign all the way to the ranch?"

"No. We lost it up around Wind River."

Flood laughed harshly. "You'll have to do better than that before you try airing your dirty wash around here."

Yorke stiffened. An invisible current of wildness boiled out of him. "Like hell I will," he said. "I saw enough, and I'm here to give you a warning. If that fire is your answer to that broken line fence business, I'm telling you that from now on you and every hand on the Chevron had better ride with his gun free and loose in his holster."

For a second or two Flood didn't catch the reference to the line fence. Then he remembered

Raines's account of the trouble he and Hoot Ellison had had with Yorke over the Sun cows that had been pushed back onto Sun range through the Chevron line fence. Raines had told him the story shortly after he'd returned to his duties at the ranch.

Now he faced Yorke with an anger that matched the Sun foreman's and went one notch further. He pushed the roan closer to Yorke. Strain stung like sweat on Flood's face. But he was hot and reckless and ready to force the issue to a showdown.

"I've got just two things to say to you, Mike. The first is that I know nothing about any grass fire. The second is that you can take your God-damned warnings and get out of here."

The color drained out of Yorke's features, leaving them tight and haggard. Fury beat him and slashed him and sent him clawing for his Colt.

Flood lifted himself halfway out of the saddle to send a pile-driving right-hand punch crashing flush against Yorke's chin. The Sun ramrod flipped over the cantle of his saddle and fell heavily to the dust. The gun he had drawn slid from his grasp and landed a few feet away from his outflung arm.

Flood leaped to the ground, his own gun fisted. "Get up, Mike, and climb back on your horse," he said.

Yorke rubbed his bruised jaw and got slowly to his feet. Hate was a dark, bitter wine in his mouth. It flickered redly in his beady eyes. "I'll get you for this, Flood."

Flood watched the ramrod mount. Then he bent down, picked up the fallen Colt. He broke the cylinder, emptied out the loads into his palm and thrust them in his pocket. Then he handed it to Yorke.

"There's your gun, Yorke," he said with a quiet deadliness. "I've got nothing against Sam Hurst or the Sun ranch. But from now on you'll keep away from the Chevron."

Yorke shook his head with a savage vehemence. "Not me, friend. This gun is easily filled again. You'll be seeing me."

With a cruel jerk of the bridle the Sun foreman whirled the black around and galloped out of the yard.

# Fifteen

JACK FARGO had one shoulder propped against a worn gray upright of the corral while he watched Calloway and Rickard throw their saddle gear on a pair of strong-limbed geldings.

"I wish you'd give that chest wound of yours a better chance to heal properly," Fargo said.

Calloway gave a tug on the cinch strap of the rangy black he was saddling, tightened it another notch, and straightened up. "Can't do it, Jack," he said. "I've been here too long already. The rest of the bunch are waiting for me back in the Tetons."

"Let them wait."

"No." Calloway's features, gray and a little gaunt from his enforced idleness, turned wire-tight. "There's that unfinished business with Dave Flood I told you about."

Fargo moved idly away from the corral. Rickard had finished with his horse and now stepped into the saddle, sending his gimlet-eyed glance roving the eastern hills where the sun's first light was striking. Fargo said, "Suit yourself, Bill. But take it easy. Too much riding won't help your chest or your leg."

Calloway slanted a sharp glance at Fargo. "How about the limp? How long will I keep that?"

"A few weeks, maybe a month or two. Depends on how you treat yourself."

Calloway put his left foot in the stirrup and with a little grunt of effort swung himself aboard the black saddler. The sudden violent movement put the bright stain of blood behind the pale wall of skin in his cheeks.

"See what I mean?" queried Fargo. He watched Calloway fight to get his breath back.

"I'll be all right," Calloway assured him. Then his dark eyes flickered as he asked: "Change your mind about joining up with us?"

"No," Fargo told him bluntly. "I'll stick with what I've got."

"This outfit of yours would make a good way station for running stolen beef through the Tetons."

Fargo looked suddenly old and tired though he was a man in his early forties. There were deep-carved lines under his eyes and at the corners of his mouth. He shook his head slowly. "I've had all the trouble I want. You did me a favor once, and I reckon I've done you one. That's as far as I can go."

Calloway sucked his lips between his teeth. A brief unpleasantness shadowed his face beneath the brim of his sombrero. "All right, Jack," he said. "I reckon it's time to drift then."

He looked at Rickard. The latter nodded curtly, lifted his reins, waved an arm at Fargo, and started down the slope from the corral.

"So long, Bill," said Fargo. "So long, Nap."

Calloway kicked his black into motion. He drew up beside Rickard. Then they hit the wide stretch of the weed-littered yard. Around the side of the long ranch house they turned to wave to Fargo and afterward sent their horses into a fast, ground-eating canter.

They rode all day, stopping once in mid-morning to give Calloway a chance to climb down from the black and walk the stiffness out of his joints, and again at noon to make a dry camp while they wolfed down the cold beef and biscuits Fargo had given them to take along. Twice more in the long, hot afternoon they made brief halts as the pace took its heavy toll of Calloway's flagging energy.

Finally, an hour before dusk, they rode into the camp where Flood had surprised Calloway and Trotter. A red-haired man called Rudley and his five hardcase companions that Rickard had hired before the fight with Flood were hunkered around a small blaze, eating beans and bacon. A pot of coffee steamed on the coals.

Rudley jumped up. "We were wondering if you'd show up today. How are you feeling?"

Calloway grimaced. "Fair. That's a damned hard ride from Fargo's place."

He got down stiffly from the saddle. His left leg buckled as he walked toward the fire, and he fell to his knees. Rudley helped him up. Calloway pushed him away. "I'll be all right. The damned leg stiffens up on me in the saddle." He looked at the fire, nodded to the other men who sang out assorted curt greetings. "Some of that coffee will go good."

A tin cup was passed to Calloway. One of the men lifted the pot from the fire and poured the cup full. Rickard, too, took a cup. Both men drank it down in great gulps. At a gesture from Rudley one of the outlaws tossed some more bacon into the pan and thrust it into the fire.

After Calloway and Rickard had eaten, Calloway retreated a short distance from the fire and leaned his back against the trunk of a tree. "Well, how's it going? Seen anyone in these hills?"

"We've had the place to ourselves," Rudley told him. "Reckon we can go on using it as a base?"

"For a few days, anyway." Calloway glanced sharply at Rudley. "Did you scout the Chevron and Sun outfits as I told you?"

"We did better than that. We set fire to one of the Sun ranch grazing meadows and then left a trail leading toward the Chevron outfit before we cut for the Tetons."

Brutal pleasure lit up Calloway's gaunt face. "Nice work, Rudley. How did it go?"

Rudley grinned evilly. "The blaze burned up a couple thousand acres of good grass. Before long Hurst and his rannies will be looking around for extra graze. Besides, Art Jackson here"—he pointed to a slim, wizened man with close-cropped blond hair and shifty eyes—"spotted one of the Sun riders pounding the trail for the Chevron after they finally got the fire out."

"Did he follow the rider?" Calloway asked.

"No," said Rudley. "But you can draw your own conclusions. My own guess is that the Sun puncher was all primed to lay the blame for that fire at the Chevron outfit's door."

Calloway slammed a fist into his palm. "That's just what we want," he said. "Peck away at both outfits until they're at each other's throats. Then, while they're gunning for each other, we'll run off their cows."

"And Dave Flood?" Rickard inquired from beside the campfire.

"He'll get his, Nap," snapped Calloway. "It's in the cards. But I'm saving him till last. I aim to make him do some squirming first."

"Meanwhile, our next move is against the Chevron, I suppose," said Rickard. "What'll it be? Another grass fire? Or a hit-and-run raid on one of their beef herds?"

Calloway considered Rickard's questions a moment. Then he replied musingly, "A raid is our best bet. But we'll only take a few head of cattle. The main thing will be to make it look as if the Sun bunch are responsible. If we could get our hands on a couple of Sun saddle ponies we could shoot one and drop the critter somewhere along

186

our escape trail." He paused and looked at Rickard. "I'll leave that job to you and Rudley to figure out."

Rickard's brows drew together. His eyes in the flickering firelight looked suddenly bright and intense. "What about you? Aren't you riding with us?"

"Not for a while," said Calloway. "I'm beat up. Fargo was right. That leg is giving me too much hell." He stopped and looked around at the staring, hard-eyed faces about the fire. "While you gents handle the riding end of it, I'll make my headquarters in Capricorn."

Rickard jumped to his feet. "Are you crazy, Bill? You can't go into town. If Flood rides in the game will be up. You'll have to fight him. There'll be no delaying."

"He never was one to go into town much. Besides, you gents will be keeping him and the rest of the Chevron hands busy hunting stolen cow critters. As for me, I reckon town is the only place. For a while I'm going to do my sleeping in a bed instead of on the ground rolled up in a saddle blanket."

Rickard took a turn up and down in front of the fire. When he came back he faced Calloway, who was still propped against the tree trunk. "What do you figure on doing in town besides sleeping in a hotel bed?"

Calloway caught the malice in Rickard's tone

and grinned. "Don't worry, Nap. I'll do my share. If everything goes as I plan I'll get myself a job as a deputy sheriff in Capricorn."

"That's the craziest scheme I've heard of yet," Rickard said.

"You wouldn't think so if I told you I was once a marshal in a small New Mexico cow town. That was before the law caught up with me and shoved me into Yuma Prison over in Arizona."

Rickard's features twisted with incredulity. "That's kind of hard to swallow, Bill."

"Maybe so, but it's true. I was a marshal for about six months. It was a nice thing I had too. I was working hand in hand with a slick bunch of rustlers. Every time there was a raid on one of the ranches I saw to it that the posse that went after the rustlers followed a dead-end trail. Then one day the whole thing blew up in my face and I had to pull up stakes fast."

Calloway chuckled at the memory of that long-ago occasion. He tapped the flap pocket of his flannel shirt. "I've still got my credentials. They're a little dog-eared and wrinkled but still good enough to fool the average cow-town sheriff. All I have to do is change the date on the papers and make it appear they were issued last year sometime."

Rickard thought of another obstacle. "Suppose the sheriff in Capricorn doesn't need any deputies?"

Calloway shrugged. "I'll worry about that when I get there. If I can't work it out I'll try something else. In any event, I mean to make my head-quarters in town. That way I can keep in touch with news on the ranges." He gestured to Rickard. "You can contact me every few days in town—but make it at night. The rest of you stay in the hills. It'll be safer that way."

"Hell," said Rudley irritably, "we like a good time in town too. What about some whisky?"

"There'll be plenty of opportunity to blow yourselves to a good time after we make our cleanup. Right now I want you gents in the hills. The only one who's to come to town is Rickard. And that's an order. As for liquor, Rickard can bring a few bottles out from Capricorn when he makes his first trip."

Then Rickard had another question. "Where'll I look for you?"

"Just check the saloons," Calloway told him. "But when you walk in don't look at me and don't let on we know each other. Step up to the bar, order a drink, then duck out again. I'll join you in a few minutes and we'll go off somewhere alone to palaver."

"I still think you're a plain damned fool and taking a hell of a risk," said Rickard. "But if you want it that way, go ahead. Only, let's have some action soon."

"And the sooner the better," added Rudley.

"We're not making any money squatting on our hunkers up here in the Tetons."

"Just give me a couple days in town," said Calloway. "You'll get action. When we're finished here I aim to have the Chevron and Sun outfits swept clean of cows."

# Sixteen

THE sun was near its zenith the next day when Calloway jogged his black gelding down the rutted main street of Capricorn.

Only a handful of chaps-clad men were visible in all the street's length. Two were seated in barrel chairs on the hotel porch, their booted feet propped on the railing. Another lounged in the black maw of a livery stable fifty yards farther on. A fourth was loading supplies onto a buckboard from the general store's loading platform.

Calloway rode past the hotel, conscious of the intently curious glances of the two loungers on the porch. Beyond the hotel he came upon a saloon, a harness shop, a blacksmith shop alive with the shrill clang of a heavy hammer striking an anvil, then a second saloon, and finally the sheriff's office and jail.

Two horses were racked up in front of the last saloon, their tails switching endlessly at the flies. Calloway noted that all that remained of the hitch rack in front of the jail were two locust uprights. The crosspiece lay in two jagged sections at the edge of the plank sidewalk.

Wondering idly if the sheriff's horse was one of those tied to the saloon hitching rail, Calloway climbed down and looped the black's reins about the bar. He ducked under the rail, then stamped up to the bat-wing doors. The dull ache in his left leg still caused him to limp.

Inside, just one man leaned against the bar. By that Calloway concluded that one of the saddled horses belonged to the sheriff.

Calloway ordered a whisky and downed it at one gulp. He signaled for a second. This he nursed along for a few minutes, warming to the heat of it in his belly. At last he finished it, tossed some change down on the bar, and limped outside again. This time he moved straight to the sheriff's office.

His first glimpse of the lawman was of a long-bodied man in black trousers, soiled gray shirt, and a worn cowhide vest. A battered star was pinned to the vest. The sheriff raised a round, saddle-leather face from the folds of an old newspaper to fix his watery gray eyes on the stranger in the doorway.

"I reckon you're the sheriff of Capricorn," said Calloway.

"You reckon right," responded the lawman. "The name is Marv Blackwell. What can I do for you?"

"I'm looking for a deputy's job."

Blackwell's gray-black eyebrows slid upward. "Not much need for more than one badge toter in a town of this size."

"Things can change mighty sudden sometimes."

"Sure they can. But I don't look for trouble."

Calloway's lips quirked. An odd glow lighted his eyes. "Maybe you'd like a look at my credentials—just in case of an emergency." He drew a folded square of paper from his shirt pocket and tendered it to the lawman. Blackwell took it with some reluctance and opened it out.

"Name's Bill Crandall, I see," he observed. He read on. "What made you quit the job down in Rincon, New Mexico?"

"Just an economy move instituted by the town council," Calloway told him. Only that morning he had carefully changed the date on the papers. "Since then," he went on, "I've been punching cows on a number of cattle outfits."

"For an outdoor man you look kind of pale," the sheriff said.

"Just got over a spell of sickness and I'm anxious to get back in harness again."

Blackwell looked him over carefully. Calloway wondered if the lawman could have some old reward dodgers about him in his desk, but he was banking on his change in appearance since then. His hair, once long, was now clipped short. His face was gaunt and thinner than it had been, and the burn he had suffered from falling in the campfire had left a faint, ruddy scar on his cheek.

"There's just nothing here for you," the sheriff said at last. "I haven't needed a deputy in the last three years. If you want work I suggest you try one of the ranches in the foothills. The Chevron or the Sun outfits might be needing somebody."

"Thanks," said Calloway gruffly. "Maybe I'll give them a try." He started through the doorway. His glance took in the drowsing horses at the hitch rack and his eyes changed abruptly, becoming shrewd and veiled. "That's a nice horse you've got out there," he said.

"That gray?" Blackwell queried. "He's just a spare mount and a crowbait at that. My regular saddler is getting new hind shoes. He's a high-spirited bay with a white blaze on his forehead and I paid a pretty piece for him."

Once on the sidewalk a slow grin spread across Calloway's face. He wasn't giving up on that deputy job—not yet, at least.

He got a room in the hotel, washed up, and changed his shirt, then spent the rest of the day on the hotel porch. After supper he had a few drinks in one of the saloons, where he learned that Sheriff Blackwell did not have his living quarters behind his office. Instead, he had a small frame house about a mile outside of town and was in the habit of riding home for a cooked meal at noon and in the evening.

It was after Calloway emerged from the hotel dining room where he'd had supper that he saw the sheriff ride out of the blacksmith shop on the blaze-faced bay. The sheriff hadn't been exaggerating. The horse was full of spit and fire.

Calloway's grin widened as he watched the sheriff disappear down the road in a cloud of dust. Then he strolled off along the deep, pitted ruts until he reached the outskirts of Capricorn, where on a small slope he found a few stunted trees and some buckthorn bushes.

Calloway pulled off a few sharp thorns, thrust them in a pocket of his levis, then went back to the hotel and went to bed.

In the morning he had breakfast in the hotel dining room and took up his station on the hotel porch. He saw the sheriff ride up on the blaze-faced bay and rack the pony in front of the saloon. The sheriff vanished inside his office.

Later in the morning Calloway limped down to the livery barn, had his own horse saddled, and took a short, aimless ride north of town. He returned fifteen minutes before noon. This time he racked up his pony alongside the blaze-faced bay. Standing between the two horses, he swiftly slid a hand into his levis, drew out one of the thorns in his pocket and wedged it under the bay's saddle. The animal reared and rolled a fierce eye at Calloway. He spoke soothingly to the bay and moved out under the hitching rail to the walk.

At noon, when the sheriff came out of his office, Calloway was at the saloon bar near by. He heard the hard clatter of hoofs, then a sudden frenzied shout. Slamming his whisky shot glass on the bar, he rushed after the bartender for the bat-wing doors. Behind them another pair made a similar dash from the far end of the bar.

Outside they found the bay bucking frenziedly, reins dragging in the dust. The saddle was empty. Blackwell lay writhing on the ground, clutching his left leg, which was oddly bent.

Two or three men rushed directly to the sheriff. But it was Calloway who lunged for the wildly pawing bay and managed to grab the animal's bridle. He was dragged for a dozen feet, then quieted the animal, and with a quick movement slid his hand under the saddle and removed the thorn that had sent the bay into a violent series of end-switching bucks the moment Blackwell's weight hit the saddle.

By the time Calloway had led the bay back to the hitch rack Blackwell had been carried into his office. A crowd gathered in the doorway, everybody trying to talk at once.

"I always figured that bay critter would throw Marv someday," one of them said.

"Yeah, but I never saw him buck the way he did today," another man observed. "You'd swear somebody rammed a hot branding iron on his rump the way he lit out from that hitching rail."

A cold, malicious amusement threw a sheen of light across Calloway's dark, deep-socketed eyes. He saw the men in the doorway part to admit a short, nimble-footed man with a black bag.

Most of the men were dispersed by the doctor.

But they hung around near the office, speculating about the sheriff's injuries. At last the door opened and the doctor appeared.

"How is he, Doc?" someone asked.

"His leg is broken," the doctor said shortly. "Is there a gent by the name of Crandall around?"

Calloway pushed forward. "That's me," he said.

The doctor jerked his thumb over his shoulder. "Blackwell wants to see you."

Calloway limped into the office. The sheriff was sprawled on a torn leather couch, his leg in a crude splint.

"You're playing in luck, friend," the sheriff told him. "Looks like I'm going to be laid up for quite a spell."

"I heard what happened," said Calloway, his face sober. "It's a tough break for you."

"Hell, it's my own fault," the sheriff said half-angrily. "That bay horse tries to throw me every time I top him. Only this time he really went crazy. You still interested in a deputy's job?"

"Sure."

The sheriff gestured to his desk. "You'll find a badge in the top drawer. Get it and bring it over here."

Calloway took the badge to the sheriff. At Blackwell's gesture he pinned the badge to his shirt.

"Raise your right hand," said Blackwell.

Calloway repeated the brief oath of office. Then

the doctor stepped in. "That's enough activity for a while, Marv. I want to get you home and to bed."

"But I want to talk to Crandall here and give him the lowdown on things in Capricorn."

"That can wait till later," the doctor insisted.

Blackwell nodded grumpily. "All right. Crandall, drop in to see me after supper. Anybody in town will tell you how to get to my house."

Calloway grinned and limped out of the room. The doctor came to the door and called to the crowd, "Gents, get used to a new deputy. His name's Crandall. Blackwell just swore him in."

Some of the men showed blank surprise. One or two grinned. Then there was a rush to the door as the doctor called for volunteers to carry the sheriff out of the office. Then a man was sent to the livery to hire a rig.

Calloway, his purpose achieved, walked away from the crowd and headed toward the hotel. He reached the porch, turned around once for a look at the men still bunched around the jail, then moved on. Without warning he collided with a soft body. He flung out his arms. There was a shocked gasp, then he saw he was holding onto one of the most beautiful women he had ever seen.

"Sorry, ma'am," he said, steadying her with his hands.

Melody Raines fell against Calloway's chest.

She looked up at him, taking her time about moving free from his arms. "Are you in the habit of walking without watching where you're going?" she asked.

A tough, twisted grin pulled at Calloway's mouth. "No," he said, "but it's a habit worth cultivating if it brings me face to face with a pretty woman like you."

Melody felt the bold challenge in the man's glance. It awoke a slow, answering ardor in her. For a good-looking man was always a keen stimulus to her quick-trigger emotions. Always she found sensuous excitement in the prospect of a new man in her life. It sparked her predatory instincts.

Ruggedness was written all over Calloway. Power and arrogance were in the set of his chin and the wide thrust of his shoulders. And somehow the bold, almost cruel way his dark eyes surveyed the curves of her body brought a secret thrill to her.

"You're a stranger in town," Melody said. "I don't recall seeing you before."

"It's my loss that I didn't come sooner," he said. And to himself he was thinking, *A damned pretty filly and she looks ripe for the picking. If I play my cards right I ought to have some fun.* Then he added aloud, "By the way, my name's Bill Crandall."

"And mine's Melody Raines."

Calloway's eyes flickered momentarily. Then he said with sudden emphasis, "The name suits you."

A little color slid into Melody's cheeks and she thought, *I'll have to be careful with this man. He moves fast. And every time he looks at me I feel as if he's undressing me.* The studied insolence of his eyes, the invisible current of turbulence that eddied around him, was a magnet completely arresting her.

She said a little breathlessly, "What is all the excitement in front of the jail?"

"The sheriff's horse just threw him."

"Was Blackwell hurt?"

"Broken leg. He'll be laid up for a spell." Calloway pointed to the badge on his shirt. "I'm deputy and acting sheriff now."

Melody smiled. "That's your good luck, then."

"Meeting you was better."

"Please," she said. "I'm a married woman." Her voice was arch and she gave him the full impact of her heavy-lidded eyes.

Calloway rocked back and forth on his heels. "Does it make any difference?" he asked.

Melody pretended to be shocked. Then she saw the crowd begin to break up at the jail, some of the men wandering toward the hotel. "I'd better be getting home—to the Chevron," she said.

"Would you mind if I tagged along? Most of this country is new to me. Maybe you could show me the points of interest."

Melody said regretfully, "It would be nice. But what will the town think if I ride out with a stranger?"

"Does it matter?"

Her eyes met his fully. The dark, bold challenge was there again in Calloway's glance. It taunted her, dared her to go along with him.

"All right," she said, feeling the heavy surge of excitement grow in her. "My horse is in front of the general store. Meet me there."

He let her pass, then turned to watch the provocative swing of her lithe hips, the supple and muscular rhythm of her thighs. With a sly, contented grin he went to his black gelding, untied it, and climbed into the saddle.

Melody was mounted on her pinto mare when Calloway reached the general store. A few idle glances from townspeople followed them out of town. Calloway paid no attention.

They rode in silence for fully a mile with the trail lifting steadily toward the foothills. Finally Melody spoke. "I've never done anything like this before."

Calloway favored her with a lopsided grin. "You're riding with the law. Nothing could be safer than that."

"I wonder," Melody said. Suddenly she laughed. It was a light, lilting sound in the warm afternoon stillness.

"Is any woman safe with a man like you?"

"That depends on the woman." Calloway's eyes took their slow, bold fill of her. "I'll wager you've got half the men in the valley chasing you."

Amusement softened Melody's face. "Not quite. I'm a married woman—in case you've forgotten."

"I've no use for your husband."

"Do you know Tom?" Melody's tone was startled.

Calloway said bluntly, "I'd hate any man who owned you."

She colored. "That's rather sudden."

"I'm a sudden man."

Melody's fingers tightened around her reins. This man's presence beside her was like a hot wind blowing against her. In imagination she felt his hands upon all the soft curves and hollows of her body. There was a tremendous animal magnetism about him. It was a suffocating force all around Melody.

They came to the crest of a high ridge. Melody halted the pinto and climbed down. "You'd better not ride any farther with me."

Calloway leaned forward in the saddle. "If it's your husband you're thinking about, let me do the worrying."

Melody turned her back on Calloway. "There's a fine view from here," she said. "That's all Chevron range below us. It runs clear to that low line of hills."

Calloway made no answer. But Melody heard the creak of saddle leather as he dismounted. Then he came up beside her, put his hands on her shoulders, and pulled her around to face him. "I'm not interested in views," he told her.

Melody saw the throbbing in the big blue vein that ran along Calloway's temple. Then, without warning, his mouth trapped hers in a rough kiss. He held her hard and tight against him. He took his fill of her, then let her go.

"You're all right," he said. "I'm going to like Capricorn."

Breathless and excited beyond all measure, Melody said, "I don't know why I let you do that." The slow stir of passion inside her made her abruptly afraid.

Calloway laughed. "You were waiting for it."

"That's not true," Melody protested, her eyes fever-bright.

Calloway took a quick step toward her. Melody retreated in panic. She didn't like his eyes. They were undressing her again.

"No more kisses," she whispered.

"That's what you were made for," he said, and followed her.

She kept retreating until she felt the flat edge of a boulder at her back. "Not again," she said. "I'll scream."

"Go ahead."

Calloway reached for her. She tried to slide past

his hands. But he caught her arms. A scream started in her throat, then lodged there as his mouth came down hard on hers once more.

Instantly she stopped resisting. Her mouth melted against his. Her arms slid around his neck. The hard buckle of his gun belt pressed into the soft flesh of her waist. She couldn't get her breath. But she didn't care. She was caught up in an electric frenzy that burned a fiery path along all her nerves.

Then his hand slid up to the open collar of her shirt. She felt his fingers on her throat. In that moment she got her senses back. She tore her lips away from his, pushed clear of him.

"No more," she said, and with a sob ran to her horse.

Calloway let her go. Violence was in him— violence like he'd never known before. But he was wise in the ways of women. He had overplayed his hand. He said, as if nothing had happened, "When will I see you again, Melody?"

Her eyes were clouded and strange. "This is the last time."

He grinned and watched her mount the pinto. "How about tomorrow afternoon same time?" he asked. "This is a good place to meet."

She didn't answer him. She was too shaken to trust herself. She dug her heels into the pinto's flanks and flashed down the slope, leaving him alone on the ridge.

# Seventeen

FLOOD was throwing his saddle gear on a big, long-gaited claybank when he spotted a fast-moving cloud of dust coming toward him across the flats. In a moment or two he recognized the rider as Hoot Ellison.

Immediately a frown corrugated Flood's forehead. Ellison and Pete Wendell, another Chevron hand, had been detailed for a few days' duty at the Wind River line camp. Ellison's instructions had been to remain at the camp until Flood sent another rider out to relieve him. The fact that Ellison was coming in to the ranch against orders could mean only one thing—trouble.

As Ellison galloped into the ranch yard, Tom Raines came out of the house and hurried to the corral where Ellison was dismounting.

"What's up, Hoot?" Flood demanded.

"We've lost some beef, Dave," Ellison said, out of breath from his hard ride.

"How many head?" Raines wanted to know.

"About fifty, near as I could reckon," Ellison answered.

"Did you pick up the trail?" Raines's voice was tense.

"Yeah, but we lost it up around that shallow stretch of Wind River."

"Hell," said Raines. "The rustlers probably hazed the critters through the water for a couple of miles. You've got to scout both sides of the river to pick up the sign again."

"I left Wendell to do that," said Ellison. "Meantime, I thought you ought to know about the raid."

"Did you get a look at the rustlers?" Flood asked.

"No. It happened sometime after midnight, I reckon. They hit the edge of that small herd we had grazing near Twin Peaks. That's quite a piece from the camp." Ellison's voice hardened. "But here's something to chew on. I picked up an old spur rowel near the Wind River shallows. The rowel had the initials M. Y. on it."

"Mike Yorke!" snapped Raines. "That jigger always did go for initials on his rowels. Hell, it reads just one way to me. Sam Hurst has made his first move against the Chevron."

"It could be a plant," said Flood.

"A plant? What are you driving at?"

"Just this." Flood's eyes narrowed. "The other day Mike Yorke rode in and told us about somebody setting fire to one of the Sun meadows. He laid the blame at our door. All of us know we had nothing to do with that—yet he claims the trail of the gents who set that fire led straight toward the Chevron."

"He could be lying," said Ellison.

"But suppose he wasn't?" persisted Flood. "Then what? Before we go off half-cocked against the Sun outfit I'd like to take a look around Wind River." He held his hand out to Ellison. "Let's see that spur rowel."

Ellison handed over the rusted bit of metal. Flood examined it closely, then passed it to Raines. "I'll bet Yorke hasn't used this rowel in years. Somebody picked it up and left it where you'd be sure to find it—somebody who maybe would like to see the Chevron and Sun ranches go to war."

Raines snorted. "That's too damn farfetched for me. Yorke and Hurst have been itching to put their grub hooks on some of our range. We've already had trouble with them, and Yorke warned me he wasn't finished. That rustled beef is his answer."

Flood shook his head. "I can see Hurst backing Yorke in a deal to grab range but I can't see him letting Yorke rustle another outfit's beef. There's something funny about this business. Give me a couple days to look into it, Tom. Then if it appears that Yorke and Hurst are really out for bear we'll swing into action."

"All right," agreed Raines reluctantly, "but I still don't like it. If Yorke gets the idea we're ready to lie down, he'll pull out all the stops."

Flood tapped his holstered gun significantly. "Leave Yorke to me, Tom. Meanwhile, it might be wise to look around in town for a couple more ranch hands."

"I'll do that right away," said Raines. "You and Hoot better get back into the hills pronto."

Flood and Ellison sped out of the yard, but separated after a few miles, Ellison to ride toward the Wind River shallows to meet Pete Wendell while Flood made a brief tour of the line fence that separated a major portion of Chevron and Sun grazing land.

Flood was about five miles from the ranch when he noticed two riders on a ridge a half-mile distant. One of them was a woman. And a glimpse of the pinto mare she was riding told him the woman was Melody.

He was cupping his hands around his mouth to call out a greeting, when he saw the man lean forward, pull Melody to him, and kiss her. It was a long kiss. Immediately Flood's features whipped tight. Melody was after a man again.

She was a woman without any loyalty and utterly without faith. The fact that she was married to Tom Raines would never trouble her—unless he found out.

The two riders drew apart. Flood saw Melody look in his direction. Flood deliberately lifted his arm in a wave. Melody signaled back again after a moment of hesitation. The man, unrecognizable from Flood's position, made no motion. And when Flood held his place without moving

Melody turned away from her companion and sent her mare racing down the near slope toward Flood.

The other rider then slowly gigged away toward town.

Melody came riding up the rock-strewn slope below Flood and halted beside him. She said with blunt irritation, "Did Tom appoint you my watch dog? What are you doing here?"

Flood didn't bother to explain. Instead, he told her, "Don't buy any more trouble than you can handle, Melody."

"Let me worry about it."

"You can't keep your hands off men, can you?" Scorn whetted his words to a fine, sharp edge.

She leaned forward and smashed the palm of her hand against his face. The blow rocked him back in the saddle. "I hate you!" she said, her eyes blazing. "All you really want to know is the name of the man you saw me with. All right. It's Crandall, and he's the new deputy in town."

"Never heard of the man. What happened to Blackwell? He's always been a lone-wolf lawman."

"His blaze-faced bay threw him the other day and he broke a leg. Nothing else he could do but appoint a deputy."

"But why a stranger?"

Melody gave Flood a frigid smile. "Ask Blackwell yourself if you're so interested."

Flood lifted his hat politely and spurred away along the down-tilting ridge.

Twenty minutes later he skirted a grass-filled meadow and came to the Chevron line fence. He followed it north in the direction of the far-distant Teton ranges. Now and then he flushed up a few scattered bunches of Chevron cattle. But he found no signs of strange cows and the fence wire and posts showed no breaks. He saw no Sun cattle or riders on the Sun side of the fence.

He was about to move on toward the Wind River camp when his eyes, scouting along a slight slope, detected a gap in the barbed wire. Flood spurred the claybank forward. Reaching the gap, he saw where two of the cedar posts had been uprooted and the triple strands of wire snapped clean with a cutter. A short distance away on the Sun side of the barrier a dead cow sprawled.

There was a welter of hoof sign all around the broken section. A small bunch of cows had been hazed through the opening, then driven across Chevron grass. Flood rode up to the dead cow. One glance revealed the Sun brand. But the thing that sent a quick rush of troubled anger through Flood was the blood-spattered bullet hole in the cow's head.

He rode back to the fence. From the saddle he studied the scuffed earth, noting the hoofprints of cattle and horses. Sometime near dawn riders had pushed a bunch of Sun beef onto Chevron range.

The dead cow—lagging behind the others for some reason—had been summarily shot.

Whoever was striking at the Sun and Chevron ranches was hitting fast and hard. Flood was almost certain that the men who had raided the Chevron Wind River camp were not on Sam Hurst's payroll—and that despite the spur rowel Ellison had found. But who was responsible, then? He thought of Calloway, wounded and bloody and threatening revenge. Had Calloway come back to strike at him by touching off a range war between the Chevron and Sun ranches? Somehow it didn't seem like the man. He was more apt to set an ambush for Flood, gun him down, and clear out.

With a grim set to his long-lipped mouth Flood pushed the claybank into motion again. The gray tautness of the skin over his high ckeekbones hinted at the raw bite of rage that had settled upon him. Head down and squinted eyes riveted upon the trail of driven cattle, he rode on over the brow of a bare hill, then on across a wide expanse of bunch grass. The sign was fresh and clear and stayed that way. Suddenly Flood found himself wondering if this, too, was deliberate.

For two miles he followed the spoor of stolen cattle. Then rounding a squat, low-hanging butte that overshadowed the trail he looked up as a sibilant whir of wings filled the air. Three buzzards, ugly and bloated from recent feasting,

211

wheeled through space and took roost in some nearby trees.

The claybank rounded the bend of trail which skirted the low shelf of rocks. Then Flood hauled the gelding to a stop. Just ahead of him sprawled the torn, lacerated bodies of five Herefords. The big round circle of the Sun brand still showed on the rumps of two of the animals. Near one of the cows sprawled a young calf.

All six of the animals had been shot at close range. But the calf was still alive. It bawled piteously. Flood took out his gun and fired point-blank at the calf.

The flat, harsh echo of the shot was dwindling away in the still air when Flood heard a soft hissing sound close to his head. He twisted around just as the noose of a lass rope dropped over him, pinning his arms to his sides. He tried to fight free, but the rope tightened cruelly and with a vicious jolt he was lifted out of the saddle.

# Eighteen

THE ground rose up beneath Flood and smote him between the shoulder blades, spilling all the breath out of him. He lay there, stunned and unmoving, the dust from his fall drifting around him in lazy spirals. At last he wrenched his body around. His eyes centered on the white-stockinged legs of three horses, then traveled up to the figures of the men in the saddles. The first rider he recognized was Mike Yorke. Immediately he struggled to his knees, fighting the stricture of the rope that held his arms pinned to his sides.

"Don't move, Flood," Yorke rasped. "We've got you dead to rights."

Beside Yorke were two grim-faced Sun hands. Each one held a gun. Flood looked down at his own Colt, lying in the loose dust where it had fallen when he was roped from the saddle.

"Get this rope off me, Mike," Flood told him.

"The rope stays where it is," said Yorke, his rugged features filled with pent-up savagery. "You've just shot your last Sun cow."

"Sure I shot it. The critter was dying when I found it."

"And what about the others you and your men killed?"

"You're crazy, Mike. I found them all shot the way they are."

Yorke curveted his horse backward. The sharp sudden jerk spilled Flood once more. He landed face down in the dust. When he struggled to his knees again there were two long abrasions on his right cheek and a spot of blood showed at the base of his nose. He spat out blood and dust.

"Flood," said Yorke, cruelly enjoying this moment, "you're going to spill your guts to me and the boys here or, so help me, I'm going to spill them for you by giving you a ride at the end of my rope."

All of the man's animal instincts were aroused. For Yorke there was a neurotic pleasure in brutality.

Flood looked at him and saw how slim his chances were. He didn't have to be told what would happen if Yorke spurred his horse into motion. He had once seen a green cowhand killed that way. All that had been left of that puncher was a splintered mass of flesh and bones.

"If you're hunting information about how these cows of yours got onto Chevron range, I can't help you," Flood said.

The nostrils of Yorke's flat nose moved in and out. The bright metal strike of temper glittered in his eyes. "Maybe you'll change your mind about talking after I bounce you over a few rocks."

Tiny beads of sweat appeared on Flood's forehead. He knew he didn't have much time.

Yorke was crowding himself to the thin edge of slaughter.

"Use your head, Yorke," Flood said sharply. "If we wanted to steal Sun cows would we leave a broad trail that even a blind man could follow? Just a little while ago I found a break in the line fence. One of your cows had been shot near the fence. The trail sign led in this direction. When I got here buzzards were already feasting on some of the critters. They'd been dead for hours."

"Yeah, and every damned one of them with a bullet hole in it," growled Yorke. "By God, I've seen enough. You and Raines aren't satisfied with hogging all that government range up around Wind River. You want every damned foot of grass in the country. That fire in our west meadow was the first step, and now this."

Time was fast running out for Flood. He saw it in the tightening of the faces all around him. The boundary between life and death for him was nothing but a thin thread, and even now that thread was straining.

Flood made one more attempt to reason with the anger-crazed foreman. "Can't you see a pattern behind all this?"

"Pattern?" Yorke's brows knitted. "What do you mean?"

"First one of your meadows is fired and a plain trail left for you to see—a trail that leads straight toward the Chevron. Then one of your cattle herds is rustled. Again the trail goes toward the Chevron. Everything points to the fact that we're trying to bust up the Sun outfit."

Flood saw that he had caught Yorke's attention. "Here's something else," he added. "A raid is pulled on one of our herds today and right where the cattle are hazed into the Wind River shallows Hoot Ellison finds a spur rowel. A rowel with your initials on it. What do you make of that?"

Yorke's full cheeks seemed to pad out. His skin turned ruddy with rage. "For one thing," he said, "you're a damned liar. For another—"

Flood cut in before Yorke could go on. "Don't you see that somebody is deliberately stirring up trouble between our two outfits? That's the only thing that makes any sense."

Yorke straightened up. His eyes were utterly cold. Flood knew suddenly that the killing moment was at hand. The hot smell of evil quivered in the air. Flood set himself, waiting for Yorke's move.

"I've heard enough," Yorke muttered. "You asked for a taste of hell the other day when you knocked me off my horse." He gestured to the dead cows. "Now you're going to see how Sun ranch skins its own skunks."

He whirled his horse around. The animal's lunge threw Flood face down in the dust. He felt the rope draw tight around his arms before he was dragged roughly forward over the uneven ground.

The rocks and gravel beneath him were like a hot branding iron searing his face and chest. His body turned into one vast pain.

Then a shrill cry rang out and he skidded to an abrupt halt in the dust as the pull on the rope slackened.

"Stop where you are, Yorke, or I'll put a rifle slug between your shoulder blades!"

Nell's voice! Yet Flood told himself that it couldn't be. He clambered awkwardly to his knees. Through a reddish mist of pain and blood he saw Nell standing beside her horse atop the low, flat butte that overhung the trail. A Winchester rifle was crooked in her arm. The long, shiny barrel was centered on Yorke's chest.

The Sun ramrod, caught flat-footed, roared at the man beside him. "Gorham, what's holding you back? You've got a gun."

"One move from any of you," said Nell, "and Yorke gets the first bullet."

But Nell's taut, unwinking stare and the ugly look of the rifle in her hands drove all thoughts of a sneak draw out of Gorham's head.

"Drop your guns, both of you!" Nell shouted to Gorham and the other Sun puncher with Yorke.

"Damn you, Gorham!" Yorke raged. "One shot would have done it."

"Maybe," said Nell grimly. "But you'd be a dead man." She turned her head a trifle and her voice softened. "Dave, are you all right?" She

217

waited for his silent nod. Then she snapped at the two Sun punchers. "Drop those Colts!" To Yorke she said, "Loosen up that rope."

With a lurid oath Yorke untied from the horn. Once the tension was eased Flood was able to free his arms and slip the noose over his head. He glanced up at Nell. "Thanks, Nell," he said. "You picked the right time to show up."

Slowly he turned from the girl and started walking toward the Sun ramrod. He reeled a little in pain and his vision still wasn't entirely clear. One thigh was badly bruised from a sharp thrust of rock. His levis were torn at the spot, and blood from a deep cut had stained the fabric. His face, too, smarted under its coating of dust.

He kept going until he reached Yorke's horse. Hell was in him now. He had been pushed too far, and for this moment he was without mercy. His hands and arms ached. But it was not an ache of pain. It was an ache of desire—the desire to crush and smash and maim the man who sat in the saddle above him.

"Yorke," he said, "nobody can do what you just tried to do to me and get away with it." His words were cold and flat and deadly. "Now I'm going to take you apart with my bare hands."

Yorke's lips skinned back against his teeth. Then Flood leaped at him. He caught Yorke's shirt in one fist and pulled him out of the saddle. He ducked a wild swing from the ramrod, then planted a hard-boned fist on Yorke's nose and felt the cartilage crush under the force of the blow. Blood sprayed from Yorke's smashed nose. It was on Flood's knuckles when Flood came in again and knocked him sprawling with a right to the jaw.

Yorke rose slowly, shaking his head like some shaggy, wounded beast. He drew his right shirtsleeve across his bleeding nose. Then he charged Flood. Head down, he rammed full tilt into Flood. The force of Yorke's assault knocked Flood off his feet. He went over backward with Yorke falling on top of him and flailing him with both fists.

They rolled over and over in the dust, sledging at each other with rope-calloused hands. A slanting blow to the corner of Flood's left eyebrow drew blood. He took another blow in the mouth, and the jar of it seemed to loosen all the teeth in his lower jaw.

Yorke's thumb jabbed at his eyeball. A sharp-edged fingernail cut Flood's eyelid. In savage anger he struck at Yorke's Adam's apple with the flat edge of his hand. Yorke gagged for breath. His hands dropped away from Flood. Instantly Flood shoved the Sun foreman off his chest and scrambled to his feet.

A thin trickle of blood filtered into Flood's eye from his gashed lid. It dimmed his vision. But he saw enough to set himself for Yorke's second wild rush. The Sun foreman came at him with both arms swinging like windmills. Flood ducked under a high left, came in close to Yorke, and buried a sharp left-hand uppercut in Yorke's midsection. Yorke gasped in anguish. He bent over, arms still pumping. Flood measured him with another left and missed as Yorke weaved away from the blow. Yorke bulled his way past Flood's guard, taking a jab to the top of the head that nearly cracked one of Flood's knuckles. Then Yorke's arms clawed around Flood's middle. There was tremendous strength in the man. He lifted Flood off the ground, whirled him around once, then flung him away. Flood struck the ground with a horrible bone-shaking thud. He heard a roar from Yorke, saw the man's rush. Then in the next moment Yorke was above him, his sharp-heeled boots canted toward Flood's chest. Desperately Flood twisted away. But he was not quite fast enough. One boot tramped down upon his left shoulder.

Hot shards of pain ripped through the ravaged sinews of Flood's shoulder. He was only dimly conscious of Yorke falling off balance away from him. The Sun foreman fell flat on his face in the dust. But Flood was too spent to take advantage of Yorke's position. By the time he got to his feet Yorke was ready for him and coming at him a third time.

Flood met the charge with his guard up high. He

took a blow high on his numb left arm. Another blow crashed through and found his midsection. The force of the punch drove the breath from him. His counter was weak and Yorke pushed in close, finding Flood's jaw with a looping right that rattled all the teeth in his mouth.

Pain was a bright red whirl all about Flood. He saw the ugly glitter of Yorke's eyes. A terrible, fanatical light burned through the grime and dust on his rugged face. He threw himself again and again at Flood, beating him back across the trail and on toward the weed-cluttered rim of a small creek.

A savage right to the point of Flood's chin dropped him to the ground. His jaw felt unhinged. There was a far-off din in his ears. Yorke drove his boot toe against Flood's shinbone. With splinters of agony spearing the entire length of his calf, Flood lay prone, fighting nausea and desperately trying to marshal his waning strength.

Out of the corner of his good eye Flood saw the sharp-edged rock gripped in Yorke's right hand. He saw the hand rise. He saw his own death in that rock. And his pain-lulled will to live asserted itself. He wrenched to one side, caught Yorke's descending arm, stopping the rock within an inch of his head.

It was Yorke's use of the rock that turned the tide of their fight. Until that instant Flood had been taking a cruel beating. But Yorke hadn't been satisfied with the use of his fists. He wanted to destroy his rival quickly, crush out his life, smash him to pulp. It touched off a wild, explosive rage in Flood that turned him as cruelly violent as Yorke.

Now, with his right hand still locked around the Sun ramrod's right wrist, he brought up his legs beneath Yorke's belly and thrust them outward with all his strength. The rock spilled from Yorke's hand. He scrambled for it, half-rising to his knees. Flood raced over, tramped on his hand. Yorke howled in pain, then started to his feet. But Flood's right knee rammed the point of his jaw and drove him back to earth again. Flood jumped on top of him, got a fistful of Yorke's shaggy hair, and lifted his head up and down, up and down, in a wicked, rhythmical beat, pounding the sun-baked earth with it.

Then Yorke broke the hold and wrenched away from Flood. The Sun ramrod got up. But this time it was Flood who charged.

Suddenly all steel, Flood kept boring in. He slashed Yorke with long lefts. And every punch was thrown with all of his weight in it. Yorke began to reel. Blood seeped from a gash in his mouth. One eye was closed, the other puffed and bruised.

At the edge of the creek bank Flood smashed him with a looping right. Yorke went down, rolled down the slight slope, and landed in the water. In the shallow creek his body lay half-submerged and unmoving.

Head down, tangled hair hanging in his face, Flood stood there drawing air into his lungs. His body was one great, punishing ache. He waited for Yorke to stir, and when the Sun ramrod still remained sodden and limp he bent down and dragged him clear of the water.

Then he caught Yorke under the ribs, lifted him half over his shoulder, and staggered up the shaly slope of the creek bank.

Through the screen of dust-grimed hair that hung across his face he saw that Nell had come down to the flats and still held the two Sun punchers at bay with her rifle.

Flood carried Yorke to the Sun punchers, then flung the ramrod roughly to the ground. "He's all yours," he said gruffly. "Take him back where he belongs and get moving."

Neither Sun hand said a word. They moved forward, caught Yorke by his shoulders and ankles, and carried him to his horse. They lashed him to the saddle, then mounted their own ponies and rode off around a bend in the trail.

Flood watched them till they were out of sight. "When they had gone the deep-seated weariness that was in him washed up and over him in a warm black tide. The top of his head seemed to lift away. He would have gone down if Nell hadn't caught him in her arms.

"Oh, my darling," she said, "you're hurt!"

The sound of her voice rallied him. He stiffened, and his pain-glazed eyes saw a warmth and ardor in Nell's glance that hadn't been there in a long time. Suddenly her mouth came against his bruised lips, and the taste of blood and dirt was somehow good and right to her.

"Dave," she whispered frenziedly, "I'll never let you go again. I don't care about Melody or anyone else. I—I thought I could hate you. But I—I can't." She kissed him again.

"I love you," he murmured against her hair.

Tenderly she slid the palm of her hand along the rugged plane of his cheeks. "Your face—it's all bruised and your eyebrow is cut. Let me clean you up."

"I'll be all right," he said, fighting against the lassitude that was creeping over him. "A wash in the creek will help."

He started off toward the stream. Nell put an arm around his waist and she draped one of his arms over her shoulders for additional support. They stumbled down the shaly bank, stopping at the water's edge. Nell helped Flood off with his shirt. Then he eased himself face down on the bank and dipped his head into the shallows.

The shock of the cold water cleared his senses and started the cut over his eye to hurting again. He scrubbed his face vigorously, splashed water on his chest. The hot sun soaked into his skin, white below the tanned line of his neck. Ruddy bruises pockmarked the flesh where Yorke's fists had found their mark.

He dried himself quickly with his stained shirt, then slipped it on again. There was a great soreness all over his body now, but some of the weakness had left him. As he turned to Nell and they climbed to the top of the bank he asked, "What brought you here?"

"I was just out riding," she replied. "I heard a gunshot. It came from the neighborhood of these buttes so I rode over."

"A good thing you did."

Nell lifted a worried face to him. "What's it all about, Dave?"

"I can't tell—yet," he said. "But I mean to find out." In a few brief sentences he told of finding the broken line fence and following the trail of the Sun cows. He finished with an account of Yorke and his men coming upon him as he shot the wounded calf, and added a word about his suspicions concerning some unknown third party trying to start a range war between the Chevron and Sun outfits.

"But who could it be?" Nell demanded.

"If I knew that I'd know my next move," he told her. "But this I do know. We're going to need some extra hands to guard our beef. Let's get back to the ranch and see if your uncle had any luck in town."

Nell glanced toward the clearly marked trail of stolen Sun cows. "What will you do about those cattle?"

"Since they're not our critters I reckon they'll have to wait. Right now I'm worried about the Chevron. I've a feeling this is only the start of bigger trouble to come and I'd like to be prepared for it."

# Nineteen

BACK at the Chevron ranch Flood and Nell found Tom Raines offsaddling near the corral after an unsuccessful trip into Capricorn. But Raines's failure to obtain additional cowhands was forgotten in his anxiety over the broken line fence and the dead Sun Herefords.

"That Yorke is an Indian," Raines growled. "You should have killed him when you had the chance."

"It wouldn't help our trouble here," Flood told him.

Raines scanned his ramrod's swollen face, the half-closed left eye. "That must have been a fight. But watch yourself from now on. Yorke isn't one to forget." Then Raines returned to the main issue. "The way I see this thing," he said, "is that Sam Hurst is looking for an excuse to go to war."

"You're wrong, Tom."

Raines shook his head. "Hell, that fire they talk about could be a plant. And how do you know Yorke and his rannies didn't smash that fence themselves and shoot a few of their own cows so they'd be able to blame us for it?"

"Yorke doesn't work that way, Tom. You know that. He's direct. If and when he's ready for battle he'll come smoking without any tricks. Somebody else is behind this—somebody that wants to see our two outfits destroy each other."

"Hell, the only other outfits around here are a few small hill ranches. They wouldn't have the guts to try anything like that." Raines's jaw worked convulsively. "I say let's round up the boys and take a pasear over to see Sam Hurst."

Flood pulled Raines back as the Chevron owner started toward the corral gate to rope out a fresh horse. "Wait, Tom! If we go busting over there you know what'll happen. There'll be blood spilled."

Raines whirled around, his heavy features truculent. "Sure and most of it will be Sun blood. They're asking for it."

"I still think it's somebody else," Flood insisted.

"Name somebody, then, damn it!"

Flood frowned in concentration. "Only one I can think of now is that renegade who tried to frame me into that bank holdup."

Nell, who had been a silent listener to their conversation, now suddenly broke in. "But, Dave, you said you left him badly shot up in the Tetons."

"I did. Two bullets went into him. If he's alive he won't rest until he takes another crack at me. He's a crazy man when it comes to revenge." Flood stopped and shook his head. "No, it can't be. After the way I left him in the Tetons he'd be in no shape for this kind of business."

Raines smacked the palm of his hand against the top rail of the corral. He was impatient. "All right. What do we do? Sit on our hunkers and just let things happen?"

"No." Flood's tone was even and his face, purplish with bruises, looked harder than it had ever been. "Give me a day or two to look around. Maybe I'll come up with something. Meanwhile, I suggest we bunch the Chevron herds up near Wind River and keep a twenty-four-hour guard on them. Hoot Ellison and Pete Wendell will hole up at Wind River tonight. When the other three hands ride in set them to rounding up the beef in the south and east sections. They can camp out in the south section tonight and be ready to start moving the beef north late in the morning. That's open country without much brush so they won't have any trouble.

"Meanwhile, I'll ride into town and see if I have any luck picking up any hands. And I'll drop in on that new deputy to let him know what's happening out here."

"He's never around when you want him," grunted Raines. "I dropped in this afternoon but his office was empty. Nobody knew where he'd gone."

"When I get back, you and I can join Ellison and Wendell at Wind River. If trouble comes that's where it'll break."

"What about me?" asked Nell.

Raines said, "That's right. Can't leave Nell and Melody here alone."

"Keep one of the boys here, then."

"No," said Nell. "Let me go to Wind River with you. Don't forget I can handle a gun."

Before Flood or Raines could reply Melody rode in. One look at Flood's battered face prompted a host of questions. When she had been informed of events she, too, wanted to take some active part in the defense of the ranch. Raines, however, wouldn't hear of it, though Nell finally won his grudging permission to go along to the Wind River camp.

"Looks like you've earned your spurs," said Melody mockingly to Nell. She resented the other girl's easy competence in range affairs and she resented, too, Nell's share in Flood's adventure. She said to Flood, "Better watch out that Nell doesn't steal your job." Then she turned and walked off toward the ranch house.

After she had gone Flood went to the bunkhouse to change into a fresh shirt. When he came out he walked into the corral and roped out the roan gelding he had taken in his wild flight from Calloway's camp in the Tetons. It took him five minutes to saddle the roan, then he climbed into his seat and struck off for town.

He reached Capricorn at dusk. There was still a broad band of light in the western sky though the sun had long since set. Only a few horses stood at the hitch racks. He dismounted in front of the Hondo Saloon. As he was flipping the reins around the hitching rail he glanced toward the sheriff's office down the street. A tall, wide-shouldered man lounged in the doorway.

Again Flood was impressed by the faint note of familiarity about the man. He was sure it was the new deputy, Crandall, whom he had seen with Melody. However, in the uncertain light, patched at intervals by the yellow wash of brilliance from store lamps that filtered into the dust of the street, it was impossible to distinguish the man's features.

Flood ducked under the hitching rail and started down the walk toward the jail. At the same instant the deputy turned and went inside. Flood hurried along the walk. When he swung in through the open doorway he found the sheriff's office vacant.

He scanned the room with a note of puzzlement in his eyes. Then he stepped to the door that led to the cell block in the rear. This was unlocked. Opening it, he found the cell block empty and immediately moved down the narrow, dark corridor to the back door. This, too, was unlocked. It opened on a weed-littered yard and a ramshackle barn. Peering out into the gathering darkness, Flood saw no sign of the deputy. He stepped out into the yard and walked over to the barn. A big dun horse was in the musty enclosure.

By the light of a match Flood examined the Leaning F brand on the dun's rump. It was a strange iron, yet that was to be expected, since Melody had told him the new deputy was a stranger.

As Flood strode back to the street he wondered at the queer actions of the deputy. Had the deputy sensed that Flood was coming to pay him a visit and deliberately avoided him? The man had obviously hurried right through the building and sneaked off through one of the alleys. For some reason it appeared he didn't want to meet Flood. But, then, could he have made out Flood's features in the murky half-light that filled the street?

Flood shrugged the questions aside. On the face of it, the deputy's action made no sense, yet he realized the man might have just been going about some private business of his own.

Back in front of the Hondo, Flood studied the empty street before stepping inside to order a drink. The whisky braced him immediately and a second shot eased some of the weariness out of his bones.

There were only three other drinkers at the bar. One man was a bowler-hatted drummer. The remaining two were punchers in from one of the small hill ranches. Still anxious to find recruits for the Chevron, he moved out into the street again.

He visited the Longhorn Saloon with no better success, then wandered into a small restaurant and had a quick supper. Afterward, he moved on down the street to the Chuck Wagon, a combined saloon and dance hall. He found only two storekeepers drinking at the bar so he turned away at once.

He came out of the bat wings, walking fast, and collided with another man on his way in. For just a moment Flood had a slanting glimpse of the man's taut, harsh-grained features limned in the outflung light from the saloon. Then he bit off a curt command. "Hold fast, Rickard!"

But Nap Rickard wasn't having any. He shoved a hand against Flood's chest and pushed him away. Flood pitched backward. His shoulders slammed against the saloon wall. He saw Rickard turn and break for the dark refuge of the adjoining alley. With a fierce, angry cry Flood plunged after the outlaw.

Rickard slid around the saloon's corner wall. Then he whirled and a gun leaped in his hand, blooming redly as he fired point-blank at the great black bulk of Flood's charging figure.

Flood's leg buckled under him. He was grabbing for his Colt and fighting to stay on his feet when the leg gave way and he fell with a heavy crash.

# Twenty

AFTER Raines and Nell had gone, Melody hurried to the corral and saddled a bay mare. The fact that Raines had ordered her to remain at the Chevron was all the prompting Melody needed to take a trip to town.

With trouble hitting the ranch the irksome tedium of routine had suddenly been shattered. Melody found herself looking forward to a new, dangerous kind of excitement. Though she had always abhorred violence of any kind, she now wanted to fling herself into the midst of Raines's preparations for defense. Accordingly, Raines's rejection of her offer to help had come like a slap in the face to her. Her immediate reaction was to strike back at him by ignoring his command.

She had to get away from the Chevron if only to show Raines that he couldn't order her around like an ordinary forty-and-found cowpuncher. As she swung into the saddle she stared across the flats. Raines had told her Val Edwards, one of the Chevron hands, was due in shortly and he had instructed Melody to tell Edwards to stay close to home and keep an eye on things. But Melody had no intention of staying around to wait for Edwards. The sooner she got away the better.

She headed the mare along the trail for town since there was no other place to go. Besides, at the back of her mind was the random thought that she might meet Crandall. The idea was intriguing even though an inner voice warned her she was playing with fire. She knew what he wanted from her. He had made no secret of it. His naked wants had been clearly revealed in the bold strike of his eyes and in the savage demands of his mouth on hers during the final moments of their last meeting.

But she was in a reckless mood now—a mood brought on by the bitter realization that her marriage to Raines had been a mistake. And she was further irritated by the certitude that she would never mean any more to Dave Flood than a woman he had casually kissed. She had noted a strange new rapport between Dave and Nell when they had all gathered in the Chevron ranch yard. Watching them, she understood that the violent events of the afternoon had brought them close together again.

When she rode into Capricorn, Flood was just in the midst of his supper, so she missed seeing him. She traveled the length of the town's rutted main street and finally racked up the mare in front of a small frame building that housed Jane Givens's seamstress shop. Gazing up and down the thoroughfare, she hurried at a quick walk toward the sheriff's office.

The shades were drawn at the side and front windows, but a narrow crack of light issued from the side window which was open two inches or so to admit some air to the stuffy room. The faint drone of voices pulled her into the shadows of the alley beside the jail. She tiptoed up to the side window and peered through the unobstructed area between the bottom of the shade and the window sill.

Crandall, the deputy, was seated in a barrel chair leaning toward another man she had never seen before. The second man was pale-eyed and pale-skinned with untidy black hair and a narrow, sharp-angled jaw. He was wearing two guns, the holsters thonged tightly to his thighs. Melody had been long enough in Wyoming to recognize the significance of those tied-down gun scabbards and she speculated about the business Crandall might have with a man whose very appearance tabbed him as a gun-slick.

It wasn't long before Melody had her answer. She was actually about to move away from the window when she heard Crandall ask his visitor a crisp question—a question that honed all her senses to a keen, perceptive edge.

"Everything all set for tonight, Nap?" Crandall queried.

"Yeah, Bill," came the terse reply. "The boys are anxious to hit both those cow outfits and clear out of the Tetons. They're starting to spook up."

"They'll get action pronto. Tonight it's the Chevron. Tomorrow or the next night we'll strike at the Sun ranch." Melody saw the deputy's face contort in sardonic enjoyment. "You're sure Raines keeps his best beef at the Wind River camp?" he asked.

The stranger answered immediately. "Dead sure. I'm meeting Rudley and the rest of the boys three miles below the camp. They'll be ready to ride the minute I get there."

"Good!" snapped the deputy. "I want every cow at that camp run off and to hell with any gun guards they may have on the herd."

"Leave it to me, Bill," the other man said with a wintry grin. Then his face altered, and he said musingly, "One thing I can't figure is what's keeping those two outfits from going at each other hammer and tongs."

The deputy shrugged. "Maybe we didn't play our cards right." Then anger smoked up his eyes. "Shooting those Sun cows and leaving them on Chevron range was a damn fool trick. Anybody with brains would be leery about finding the critters like that. Flood probably smelled something wrong."

"You still saving him for yourself?"

The deputy scowled blackly. "He's my meat, and don't any of you forget it. He's going to pay for lifting that bank loot from me." He rose abruptly, pulled a watch from his pocket. He examined the face of it and frowned. "Time to pull your freight, Nap."

The stranger nodded. "Sure, just as soon as I wash down some of the dust in my throat with a little redeye."

Melody saw the deputy's scowl deepen, and when he spoke to his companion his voice was hard. "You stay out of the saloons. Flood's in town. I don't want you running into him."

The other man's features curled up in surprise. "You'd better clear out of here yourself. If he walks in on you now, you'll have your ruckus before you're ready for it. How long ago did you see him?"

"About an hour ago. I saw him dismount. He started down this way. I don't know if he recognized me in the doorway. I ducked out through the back and avoided him."

"Is he still here?"

"Wouldn't be surprised. That's why I want you to rattle your hooks out of town and get up to Wind River."

The stranger grinned at the deputy, then turned and went out the door. By the side window a slow, labored breath squeezed out of Melody's lungs. A sick, cold feeling of horror held her rooted to the spot. The things she had overheard were a startling, almost incredible revelation. They turned her narrow, circumscribed world upside down.

She felt a sudden loathing for the deputy, and she was disgusted with herself for the liberties she had permitted him to take. The man was nothing but an outlaw masquerading as a lawman. But what made his role all the more terrible was the fact that he was one of the renegades who had stolen the ranch money from Flood and had then tried to frame him into the Blue Mesa bank holdup. And now—this very night—Crandall's hirelings were planning to raid the Chevron's Wind River line camp. After that Dave Flood was scheduled to die.

It was this final shocking realization that shook Melody out of her paralysis of fear. If Flood was still in Capricorn he had to be warned about his enemies. She had to get to him before it was too late.

With a dry sob racking her throat Melody moved back to the street. But she had barely reached the plank sidewalk when a gunshot ripped the night apart. There was a split-second interval of silence, then a second shot roared out.

Melody's heart stopped beating. Again terror froze her into immobility. A coil of rope seemed to have gathered in her insides. It twined and twisted into a great, suffocating knot as she waited and heard the town of Capricorn come frighteningly alive.

Saloon doors flew open. Men rushed through yellow bars of illumination and faded away into darkness. There was the heavy tramp of boots, a strident yell. And then one man's bull-like bellow reached Melody.

"Somebody shot Dave Flood!"

Melody felt as if a sharp scalpel had slit the skin of her body, letting all the blood drain out. Panic ripped at her. She found herself crying. Flood was shot. Flood was dead. She had waited too long. The hidden scalpel kept slashing at her, tearing her apart.

Through tear-dimmed eyes she saw a black knot of men mill about in front of a saloon a block away. One or two individuals broke from the crowd and darted into an alley.

Suddenly Melody thought of the grinning hardcase who had been with the deputy. She knew as well as she had ever known anything in her life that the renegade had shot Flood. And with that knowledge some of the dread left her. She told herself she ought to go to Flood to see if she could help him. But a sudden wild impulse changed her mind.

She wanted to reach the man who had shot Flood. She wanted to kill that man—wanted to see him squirm under the bite of burning lead.

Half-blindly Melody swung from the empty walk and lurched back into the alley. She groped for the .38 revolver she carried. Her fingers closed around the walnut stock. She had never gotten over her awkwardness with the weapon. But now she didn't care. The feel of the gun against the palm of her hand stilled her chattering teeth, locked the grief deep inside her.

She paused by the window of the deputy's office. One quick glance through the narrow opening between the shade and the wooden sill showed her that the deputy had gone. She slid away, moving at a stumbling run down the alley.

When she came to the end of the jail building she found herself in a weed-littered yard. Far to the left of her, somewhere in the vicinity where the shooting had taken place, she heard a stir of movement. Men were searching for the ambusher, she told herself.

But here in back of the jail there was nothing. No sound. No movement except the nicker of a horse from the ramshackle barn.

Melody hardly knew what prompted her to go toward the barn. The man who had shot Flood was by this time well on his way out of town. Surely he wouldn't be fool enough to hide in a building so close to the jail. But there was the deputy himself—the man who called himself Crandall, the man she had heard say Flood was "his meat." Crandall, too, had to be stopped!

The horse in the barn nickered again. Melody, gun in hand, hurried through the gloom of the back street. The darkness was suddenly full of damp hands groping for her. Her skin crawled with a nameless terror. The night air turned leering and ugly. She ran toward the barn. But she couldn't escape the darkness, the eerie sense of long-reaching hands outstretched to arrest her flight. And then, in the deeper shadows of the barn doorway, she plunged into a pair of hands that were shockingly alive and real.

Panic sent a shrill cry welling up into Melody's throat. But the cry was throttled by the bony ridge of a man's arm clamping against her windpipe. A hand closed over her mouth. It shut off her breathing. For a half-minute she fought frantically to get free. But the hard hand on her mouth sealed off the air going to her lungs. Suddenly she stopped struggling. As blackness began to flood her brain she felt herself being dragged backward into the barn.

It was well after dark when Tom Raines and Nell reached the Wind River line camp. Hoot Ellison emerged from the cabin with a gun in his fist, but a quick call from Raines put the puncher at his ease.

"What luck?" asked Raines.

"None at all," replied Ellison as Pete Wendell came out of the shack with a storm lantern. "We found where that Chevron beef had been hazed out of the river shallows, but we lost the trail in the malpais four or five miles farther on. We hunted around till dark in the foothills. It just wasn't any use."

"They're high in the Tetons by now," put in Wendell.

Raines ground his teeth together. "I reckon that's so."

"Where's Dave and what's Nell doing here with you?" Ellison wanted to know.

"There's been more trouble. Dave's gone to town to see about hiring more hands. Looks like we're going to need them." Raines dismounted, helped Nell down from her mare, then turned back to Ellison and Wendell to bring them up to date on events. "Dave and I don't agree on who's behind the raids on our beef as well as Sam Hurst's cows," Raines concluded.

"It's a puzzle to me," Wendell said.

"You're putting your chips on Mike Yorke," said Ellison to Raines.

"Sure. It's just the kind of Indian trick Yorke would pull," the rancher replied. "Raid the other fellow's herd, then steal a few of your own cows to make it look as if some third party is hitting both sides. I don't buy it."

Nell, sensing Raines's quick rage, said quickly: "We've got nothing to lose by giving Dave a free hand to look around before we make a definite move."

"Nothing but more of our beef," snapped Raines acidly. "The longer we wait the worse off we'll be."

Nell protested. "But Dave's already taking steps

to cut down on the chances of another raid on Chevron beef." At Ellison's inquiring look she explained: "Dave plans to have all the cows on our south and west ranges hazed up here and kept under heavy guard."

"That makes sense," admitted Ellison, pushing his light brown unruly hair out of his eyes.

Raines said gruffly, "You boys have supper yet?"

"We were just fixing to prepare grub when you folks rode up," Ellison told him.

"All right, boys," Nell said. "That's my department."

They stepped aside to let her enter the cabin. At a nod from Raines, Wendell took the horses and led them away to the corral in back of the line cabin.

When the puncher had gone Raines said to Ellison: "We'll ride two guard shifts tonight. Nell and I will take the first trick. We'll route you and Pete out about midnight."

"You expect something may break tonight?"

"Never can tell. I just don't intend to take chances."

They had a quick supper which Nell whipped up from the well-stocked shelves in the cabin. As soon as the dishes were cleared away Ellison and Wendell prepared to turn in to get as much sleep as possible before midnight.

Raines and Nell hurried to the corral. The

rancher saddled up fresh horses. They mounted and rode away from the cabin, angling toward the grazing Chevron herd in a wide meadow a half-mile away. The meadow was hemmed in on two sides by a low line of buttes for a considerable distance. But then Wind River cut in out of a thick stand of willows, leaving the ground open and free of impediment for a couple of miles until the winding course of the stream turned in upon itself in a wide U-curve, leaving an exit only to the east over a series of low, humpbacked ridges.

The night sky was clear and awash with the crystal brilliance of myriads of stars. Low on the horizon a deep yellow glow heralded the rise of the moon. Under the star glow the Chevron cattle had a ghostly, unreal look. Even the long, curling grama grass had the weird, milky appearance of small breakers assaulting a sandy beach.

At the edge of the herd Raines halted and spoke in low tones to Nell. "We'll ride a circle around the herd, going in opposite directions. Keep a sharp lookout in the surrounding brush. If you see anything queer, fire one shot from your gun."

"Right." Nell's voice was crisp with suppressed excitement. She saw the troubled, drawn expression on Raines's face and added: "Don't worry about me."

He shook his head ruefully. "I shouldn't have let you come. This is no work for a woman to be doing."

She patted his hand. "I'm glad of the chance to help. Probably nothing will happen tonight anyway."

"I hope not," Raines replied, but his voice was dubious.

He turned his gelding away from her and rode off. Nell pushed her mare into motion and began her slow circuit of the Chevron cows. Some of them were already bedded down for the night. Others stood idly cropping long tufts of grass. The animals looked calm enough, and unless some unforeseen disturbance came up they would offer no problem to guard.

Nell found that it took thirty minutes to make a complete circuit of the herd. She passed Raines, but he had nothing to say to her. The moon came up during that time—a bright crescent that looked like a great curved scimitar in the sky.

By ten o'clock a thin screen of clouds partially obscured the moon. Off in the west the clouds lay dark and thick and formless. Out of them suddenly streaked slashing ribbons of lightning. Then came the low, dull rumble of thunder.

Riding around the far edge of the herd, Nell caught the first faint signs of uneasiness in the cattle. Many of the creatures stirred restlessly on the ground. A few rose to their feet, moving about in nervous fashion. The wind quickened, and whorls of dust flew through the air.

Nell felt a slight tremor of fear. If a storm came

up the herd could easily be transformed into a horrible engine of destruction. She had seen one cattle stampede and would never forget it—the wild, bawling terror of cows going completely berserk; the ugly clack of horns; the thunder of galloping hoofs that could crush a horse and rider, pound them into utter oblivion, if they fell in the path of flight.

Raines stopped Nell on their next circuit. "I don't like that sky," he said. "A storm could raise hell with those critters."

"It might only be heat lightning," Nell said as another vivid flash seemed to open the sky.

Raines shook his head. "If the critters don't bed down soon I'll have to rouse Ellison and Wendell. I don't want you out here if a storm hits."

He moved on out of sight. Nell shivered in a sudden blast of cool, damp air. Nearby a half-dozen steers heaved themselves off their bed ground and surged into motion. Somewhere a cow bawled in muted terror. The sound was picked up by others as a great white arrow shot across the black hummock of clouds. Afterward the sky seemed to gouge an opening in itself and red and white flashes leaped outward across the heavens.

The smell of sulphur hung in the air. Terror put a white shine on Nell's cheeks. The night throbbed to the beat of thunder and to some nameless, clinging dread. She moistened her lips with her tongue. A choking sound came from her.

It was almost a sob. To cover her own fear she started to croon to the restless cattle as she rode.

Then from the edge of the buttes a few hundred yards from Nell's position came a sudden commotion. It sounded like horsemen. She stiffened in the saddle, turned to look along her back trail. A bunch of riders appeared at the fringe of the herd. Guns boomed in their hands. Loud yells siphoned from their lungs. And in the next flash of lightning the Chevron cows were up and running.

Nell dragged out her .38 revolver. She fired two shots in the direction of the raiders, realizing at once how silly her action was. Then the massed bunch of cattle exploded outward all around her. Without any signal from Nell the mare lit out in a gallop to keep from being run down.

Panic crawled up and down Nell's spine. She was caught in a stampede. From this moment on she would have to ride as she never rode before. The Chevron beef were on the move, and they were going away from the line camp toward the river.

Nell emptied her revolver at the line of cows on her right, trying to open a passage for the mare to reach the flank of the herd. Three steers went down. Nell neck-reined her mount into the slight gap she had created. But the rush of steers from the rear closed the opening and she remained trapped.

A dread hopelessness filled her then. All around her fear-crazed cows were racing over the hard-packed ground as if the hounds of heaven were chasing them. The booming rataplan of hoofs drowned out every other noise. Dust rolled up in choking waves, yet it could not conceal the ghostly, heaving heads and shoulders of the spooked-up steers.

Nell bent low over the mare, urging the animal to its utmost speed. Yet the lunging horse was unable to break through the thin wall of cows running in front of the stampede. All of Nell's nerves knotted up in her chest. Breathing became a positive effort. She kept screaming, but the sound was lost in the din of the stampede.

A segment of the herd broke away in a tangent, cutting away from the river which now loomed up in a crystal glitter on the girl's left. But again other frightened steers moved up from the rear ranks to fill the gap, and Nell was unable to break into the clear.

Ahead of her Wind River began its long, curving arc toward the horseshoe bend. Suddenly a new terror assailed her. In swinging back upon its own course the river had formed a short stretch of stagnant backwater. During the course of years some of the water had found its way across a marshy tract of mud and sand. The area was a quagmire avoided by cows. But now, caught in a blind panic, the Chevron beef critters were headed straight toward their own destruction. And with them they were carrying Nell.

Sobs of helpless fury racked the girl. She tried to reload her gun, planning to fire at the heads of the cows nearest her to open a path to freedom. But the ragged motion of the mare and her own trembling terror made her drop the gun.

Suddenly she saw the marsh dead ahead of her and knew she was lost. Several steers close by plunged into the mud. Their piteous bawling knifed through Nell. Then the mare hit the soft, slippery footing and stopped with an abruptness that threw Nell right out of the saddle. She pinwheeled through space and landed feet first in the mud.

Hysteria flowed through her like a sheet of ice. She struggled to free her feet. But the very fury of her efforts drove her deeper into the mud. All around her the air vibrated to the bawling of frightened cows. She heard them plunge into the marsh, heard their frantic struggles, heard the loud sucking sounds of the mud as it digested its prey.

The mud was around her knees, then well past her thighs. Cry after cry tore from her tortured throat. The mud kept dragging her down and down. It was a cloying, viscous mass seemingly without bottom. She sank to her hips. Still she struggled and fought. And every move plunged her deeper into the ugly morass.

# Twenty-one

THE flash of Rickard's gun tore a bright red hole through the darkness. Flood, running fast to cut off Rickard's escape, felt the toe of his right boot snag in a broken section of the board sidewalk. His leg buckled. The momentum of his rush carried him forward and down and the heavy-calibered slug intended for his heart passed through the high crown of his sombrero.

He hit the walk with a bone-shaking jolt. But his Colt was in his fist, and he snapped a shot toward the head of the alley, afterward hearing the spent bullet slam into the frame wall of the yonder building. Scrambling to his feet, Flood lunged recklessly into the alley. He was fully aroused now and anxious to shoot it out with Rickard.

As he skidded into the narrow aperture between the saloon and the adjoining darkened store another bullet from Rickard's gun went singing by him. The outlaw had sprinted to the end of the alley. Flood drove a shot at the man's running shape and knew he had missed when Rickard kept running and vanished around the corner of the saloon.

There was an instant clamor in the street beyond Flood. Men were pouring out of the saloons with a wild stamping of feet. Flood, intent on his pursuit of Rickard, paid no attention to the noise in the street. Keeping close to the saloon wall, he ran lightly down the alley. His muscles were strung wire-tight. At any moment he expected Rickard to poke a gun around the corner of the saloon and pick him off with a snap shot. But before he reached the rear lots Flood heard the clatter of hoofs, the sound diminishing quickly. He broke past the end of the alley. A hundred yards away and racing toward a thick line of trees he saw a horse and rider. Rickard had had a saddled horse close by. Pursuit was out of the question. He was out of six-gun range, and by the time Flood got his own mount Rickard would be deep in the timber.

Flood swung around and trudged back toward the town's main street. Several men came toward him. One of them sang out, "Who's that?"

"Dave Flood. Somebody just took a shot at me."

The men, punchers from a couple of the small hill ranches at the edge of the Tetons, clustered around Flood.

"Did you get a look at the jasper?" one puncher asked.

"No."

"If you want some help rounding him up just say the word. We could do with some excitement."

Flood shook his head. "Whoever he is, he's well in the timber by this time."

He shoved his way through them and moved on to the street. Here in the outflung light from the saloon he rammed fresh cartridges from his belt loops into the two empty chambers of his Colt. Then he thrust the weapon back in the holster and went off down the walk. He was conscious of the hill rannies watching him. But he didn't care about anything except Nap Rickard and the implications of his presence in Capricorn.

Wherever Rickard was he knew Calloway could not be far away. He was suddenly sure he had his answer to the trouble that had struck the Sun and Chevron outfits.

The sheriff's office still showed a light. But a cursory examination of the front room and the cell corridor in the rear proved fruitless. Crandall, the deputy, was not around. His absence was no surprise to Flood. Bleak-faced, he stormed out of the office and hurried to his horse.

Once in the saddle he sent the roan at a fast gallop out of town. He rode a half-mile, then pulled into a narrow offshoot of the road. Following the line past a grove of cottonwoods, he came to the small frame house occupied by Sheriff Marv Blackwell.

Mrs. Blackwell, a slender, gray-haired woman in her late forties, answered Flood's knock and admitted him to the house. She showed him the way into the bedroom she shared with her husband, then left him.

Blackwell was propped up in bed, idly paging through a mail-order catalogue. He looked up at Flood's entrance.

"Hello, Flood," said Blackwell. "What's prodding you?"

"You see a lot," Flood told him. "How are you feeling?"

"Good as can be expected. I won't feel right until I can ease myself into a saddle again." Blackwell's eyes narrowed and he asked, "Seems to me I heard some shooting off toward town. Is that what you're here about?"

Flood's face grew long and hard. The lamplight picked out hard glints in his eyes. "Somebody tried to kill me tonight," he said.

The sheriff's half-open mouth snapped shut. He peered sharply at Flood. "Who was it and did you get him?"

"He got away, Marv." Flood paused briefly to emphasize his next words. "The man was one of the hardcases who held up the Blue Mesa bank."

Blackwell sat up straight. "You sure?"

"I had a good look at his face. There's no mistake about it."

"So your friends are out for your scalp."

"It's more than that," said Flood, the muscles of his rough-hewn, battered cheeks twitching under the deeply tanned skin. "Both the Chevron and the Sun have lost some beef this week. And there was a fire that ruined a big piece of Sun graze. Mike Yorke came busting over to our place ready for war. He picked up a trail that led toward the Chevron. We had nothing to do with that fire or with stealing any beef.

"This afternoon I spotted a wide break in our line fence. I also saw signs of a big movement of cattle. I followed the spoor until I came upon a bunch of Sun cows that had been deliberately shot. Yorke and a couple of his men caught me putting a wounded calf out of its misery. Yorke drew his own conclusions about that."

Blackwell nodded sagely. "Which explains the look of your face. It must have been a hell of a fight."

Flood didn't crack a smile. "It was. But forget the fight. That trail of stolen beef was a plant. So were those dead cows. You see the pattern?"

"Somebody's trying to touch off a range war between your outfit and Sam Hurst's. Your guess is that your friends from Blue Mesa are out to smash both ranches and kill you." Blackwell's mouth set and he rapped the side of the bed with his fist. "That jasper trying to bushwhack you tonight makes it add up. Better get in touch with Crandall."

Flood snapped a sharp question at the sheriff. "How well do you know that deputy?"

Blackwell's eyebrows rose in surprise. "He's pretty much of a stranger but his credentials seemed all right. He was a town marshal down in New Mexico. Why? Do you figure that—?"

Flood interrupted Blackwell curtly. "What does he look like?"

The sheriff thought a moment, then said, "He's a big man, heavy-featured. A square, blunt sort of face. Dark eyes, heavy brows, and kind of arrogant-looking. Walks with a kind of limp."

Flood snapped his fingers. "That limp settles it, Marv. You've hired one of the Blue Mesa outlaws."

"Hell, that can't be!"

"It is, I tell you." Flood's voice was hard and firm. "Crandall, your deputy, is the leader of the bunch who ambushed me in that hotel in Blue Mesa. I winged him twice in their camp in the Tetons. One of my bullets drilled his leg. And I happen to know he once was a marshal but he beat it out of town ahead of a lynch mob when the ranchers found out he was mixed up in some rustling."

Anger churned in Blackwell's face. He didn't like the idea of being taken in by a renegade. "Those credentials he showed me must have been doctored up."

"Sure. He just changed the date on them." Flood hitched up his gun belt. "All right, Marv. I found out what I wanted to know." He stepped to the door.

"You know where to look for your friends?"

"In the Tetons, I reckon. But right now I'm headed for Wind River. We're gathering all the Chevron beef in that one spot to make it easier to guard."

Blackwell frowned. "You could be saving those hardcases a lot of trouble in running them off too. One herd is easier to rustle than a half-dozen scattered all over the range."

"True enough," Flood admitted. "But with our small crew there's nothing else we can do."

"I can swear you in as a deputy. Then you can recruit as many men as you need from town."

"That's white of you, Marv. Right now I don't reckon that'll be necessary." Flood moved through the doorway into the hall. He lifted his hand. "I'll be seeing you."

He walked out to the front room, called a good-by to the sheriff's wife, and hurried out of the house. In the saddle once more, he sent the roan down the tree-lined lane at a fast run. At the end of the lane he crossed the main wagon road and swung north along a rising pitch of ground.

An hour of hard riding stretched ahead of him before he could expect to reach the Wind River camp. Deep in the west angry white ribbons of heat lightning slashed the sky. He also heard a far-off rumble of thunder. The air was cool against his face, and he wondered if the long-overdue rain would hit the range tonight.

But the heavy clouds in the west had thinned

out by the time he struck the steep slope of the last ridge that cut him off from the river and the Chevron line camp. It was then that he heard a scatter of gunshots and a few dim yells. The gunfire was followed almost at once by the bawling of cattle and the deep-toned mutter of many hoofs plunging into concerted motion.

Stampede! That one word hammered through his brain. Calloway had struck again. And the knowledge that he was too late—had delayed too long in town—filled Flood with a bitter rage. He jammed his hooks into the roan's flanks. The animal answered the summons with a burst of speed. Up and up the long, rock-strewn grade the roan galloped. And all the while the roar of the distant stampede was carried to him in one continuous rumble of noise by the cool night wind.

At the top of the ridge Flood didn't pause to let the roan blow. Again he spurred the animal, and again the roan answered with a powerful drive of its legs. Within ten minutes he sighted the line shack. The corral was empty. A lamp burned on a table inside the cabin. He saw that as he peered through the open doorway. Going past at a hard run, he had just that brief glimpse. But he knew that the stampede had pulled every Chevron man along with it.

Then a new thought assailed him. Nell had gone up with Raines to help guard the Chevron cattle.

Where was she now? Had she taken the first guard trick with one of the men? Or had she been in the cabin?

Frantic with sudden cold fear, Flood sped on across the wide meadow. The thunder of hoofs was well beyond him, going away from the camp. Interspersed with that wild din came a faint, high-pitched bawling, and then, still farther away, a flat crash of sound that could be nothing else but the crack of a gun.

Dust hung low in the air, stirred up by the passage of the fleeing steers. Flood bent low over the roan's mane, urging the animal to still greater speed. His gun came automatically into his fist. He strained his eyes through the night, searching for signs of riders or the heaving bodies of cattle.

To his left he noted the gray glitter of Wind River as it started its great U-curve. The stampede had carried off to the right. He swung the roan in that direction, then stiffened as a new sound reached him. It had the oddly familiar ring of a human cry. A shiver ran up and down Flood's back. He drew the roan down to a canter, every sense alerted to catch the sound again.

When it was repeated, he knew he had not been wrong. It was a cry—a cry of terror. He neck-reined the roan to the left, angling toward the river. The cry came a third time. At once he knew it was Nell.

"Nell!" he called stridently.

He waited tensely, the roan again pulled down to a canter, his head swinging from side to side to examine the ground.

"Dave!" The word was high-pitched, keyed to a scream.

He rode forward, the arc of the river bending back upon itself. Ahead of him he caught the glitter of water through a thin screen of trees.

"Dave!" Nell's cry was like a knife rammed through Flood's insides. "Over here. Watch— watch out!"

Flood hauled back on the reins with a sudden savage jerk as he belatedly recognized he had come to the edge of the marsh. At that moment the moon slid its white banner of light through a break in the clouds and he saw Nell buried almost to her armpits in the quagmire.

"Hold on, Nell!" he said as the roan, skidding to a halt, reared high in the air right at the edge of the bog. Flood swerved the animal around, nearly unseating himself in the maneuver. But the roan kept its footing on hard ground.

Quickly Flood jammed his Colt back into his holster and spun out his lariat.

"Dave—Dave, hurry!" the girl pleaded, her face gray and panic-stricken in the moonlight.

Flood heard a horrible wrenching sound in the mud. Far to the right a struggling cow disappeared in the viscous mass. Even as he built a loop in the lariat he saw Nell's body sink another notch. Then he flipped the loop toward the girl. The cast was straight and true. The loop dropped over Nell's head and shoulders.

"Get the rope under your armpits, Nell!" Flood directed.

The girl obeyed instantly though her movements drove her deeper in the mud. Flood sent the roan backward, tightening the noose. Then he urged the roan into motion. For a moment the mud resisted the pull of the horse. It was reluctant to relinquish its prey. But the roan leaned hard into the rope. Once again there was a great bubbling sucking noise and Nell was pulled free. The roan dragged her a few yards beyond the edge of the marsh.

Flood leaped from the saddle and ran back to the girl where she lay sprawled on the ground. Tenderly he gathered her in his arms.

"Oh, Dave, Dave!" she said in a strangled sob. She clung to him. Her fingers dug into the flesh of his shoulders. A great trembling racked her slender body. Flood held her close. He felt the warm beat of her heart against him. Then her face, tear-stained and mud-streaked, lifted to him, and he kissed her. Again she clung to him, still shaking.

When the spasm had passed she drew away. "All right now, Nell?" he asked gently.

She glanced toward the bog and shivered. "Yes," she said. "I—I thought I'd never see you again, Dave. It—it was awful. There—were—cattle all around me dying, being sucked down into the mud. The sound of the mud dragging at me and the steers was terrible."

Flood looked beyond Nell to study the empty prairie. Nothing moved out there as far as he could see. "What happened to Tom and the others?" he asked.

She said in quick concern, "I don't know, Dave. I haven't seen any of them since the stampede started. Tom and I were riding on opposite sides of the herd when a bunch of horsemen hit the steers, shouting and yelling and firing their guns. I got caught in the press of cattle and couldn't get clear." She stopped and shuddered. "Several times I thought the mare was going to stumble and go down." Her fingers dug into Flood's arms. "Dave, do you think they—they might have been caught like that?"

"Let's hope not, Nell. It's a hell of a way to die." He glanced toward the swamp. "Though not any worse than being drowned in a bog. But we ought to have a look around. A lot of things can happen when a bunch of fear-crazed cow critters start to run." He tipped Nell's face toward him. "Do you feel up to riding?"

Nell got wearily to her feet, Flood helping her. "I'll be all right," she assured him. "We'll have to travel double. My mare went down in that mud."

She paused to brush at the slimy mud that clung

to her skirt and boots. But they were beyond brushing. The skirt was ruined and her yellow shirt was wet and stained with brown mud. Flood led her to his roan and gave her a hand up into the saddle.

"You need some fresh clothes, Nell. I don't want you catching cold. Wish I had a jacket." He started to peel off his shirt.

"No, Dave," she protested. "That won't help much. I can wait till we get back home. Right now I'm worried about the others."

He nodded silently, then climbed up behind her and put the gelding into motion.

Melody fought frantically against the black wave of faintness that washed over her. Deep in the darkness of the barn she felt herself pushed back against a lump of hay. She swayed sickeningly, her shoulder striking the wall. Then a match flared in front of her. Behind the cupped flame she saw the shadowed face of the man she knew as Crandall.

"Melody!" he exclaimed. "What are you doing here?"

Anger and fear whirled in Melody's wide-spaced eyes. Her vision cleared. Strength returned to her legs. She got up, tried to dash past him. A quick lunge brought him up beside her. He caught her arm, pulled her back from the doorway. "Not so fast, Melody."

She struggled in his grasp, beating at him with her free hand. "Let me go!" she cried. "You're an outlaw—I—I know all about you." Her voice rose and she tried to scream.

Calloway clamped a palm against her mouth and pulled her roughly toward the rear of the barn. There he released her and snapped out a terse question. "What are you talking about?"

Melody couldn't see his face in the gloom, but his breath was warm on her cheeks, and the smell of cheap whisky was on his breath. She was afraid of him—afraid in a completely different sense than she had been before. It was a fear born of a thorough knowledge of his wickedness, and she wondered how she had ever permitted him to take liberties with her.

"I know all about you," she said recklessly. "You're a renegade. You held up the Blue Mesa bank the time Dave Flood was caught. And you're here posing as a lawman."

Calloway grabbed her arm. His voice turned threatening. "So you were hanging around the sheriff's office tonight."

"Yes," she replied with savage defiance. "And I saw and heard enough to tell me that you and your friends ought to be hung. You're planning to steal some Chevron cattle tonight and you also mean to kill Dave Flood." Her voice rose frenziedly. "But you won't get away with it!"

She struck at him with a small knuckled fist.

The blow cut his lip. She twisted away and ran toward the door. Calloway charged after her. She let out one frightened scream before he flung himself upon her. His arms trapped her hips and dragged her down in a heavy fall with his own body half rolling over her.

The shock of the fall knocked the wind out of Melody. She lay prone on the hard-packed earth of the barn. There was a smudge of dirt on one cheek and her divided skirt had hiked up above her knees.

Calloway looked at her closely to make certain she wasn't shamming. Then he went to his saddled horse, brought the animal to the doorway. With deft ease he picked up Melody's limp body. She stirred as he carried her to the waiting horse.

"Let me go!" she said. "Put me down."

"Sorry, Melody. You and I are going for a ride."

She clawed at him with her hands, trying to get free. "You can't make me go," she declared.

Calloway laughed harshly. "I'm afraid you don't have any choice."

He hefted her into the saddle. When she squirmed and tried to slip down on the far side of the horse, he hauled her roughly back. "I can be rough if I have to, Melody," he said. "It's up to you."

She saw the hard, inimical burn of his eyes and cowered away from him. In her moment of hesitation he leaped up behind her and sent the gelding racing out of the barn. He struck straight away from the main buildings of Capricorn. In that direction Melody heard the chatter of voices and occasionally a loud shot. She would have cried out for help, but Calloway anticipated her intention and trapped her mouth with a calloused palm. Though she fought to free herself of the restriction, his strength was too much for her. Only when they were well away from town and climbing toward the foothills of the Teton range did his hand drop away from her mouth.

For a moment Melody's first interest was to gain a breath of cool, clean air. Then she twisted in his arms and faced him angrily. "You won't get away with this," she said.

Calloway's long, thin upper lip bent in a slight grin. "I'm doing all right." He leaned closer to her, his glance intent upon the provocative curve of her mouth. "You're even prettier when you're mad."

Before Melody could stop him he had kissed her. She pulled away and scrubbed her lips with the back of her hand. "I'll kill you if you do that again," she said.

"With what?" he asked, his voice mocking her. "I can remember when you liked the idea of my kissing you. In fact, you couldn't seem to get enough of me."

Melody's anger made her wretched. "I—I hate you now. And I hate myself for having anything to do with you."

They jogged on across the top of a wide wooded bench, then plunged downward into a sinuous, shaly ravine. With the echoes of the horse's steel-shod hoofs ringing against the rocks in the dry stream bed he said, "You're going to have to put up with me for a while, Melody."

Fear struck sharply at her. She spoke tremulously. "Where are you taking me?"

"To my camp in the Tetons."

Melody faced him again. Her voice had the same pallid quality as her skin. "You can be hanged for what you're doing," she said.

He nodded, unperturbed. "And for some other things I've done in my time."

"By morning the hills will be swarming with men looking for me. Let me go, and I promise not to say anything about you to anyone. Just go and don't come back." She ended on a note of frenzy.

Calloway laughed. "You're wasting your time. If I let you go now you'd run to Dave Flood and upset my plans."

"You may get the Chevron cattle, but Tom or Dave will kill you for this."

"Your friend Flood is the only one I'm interested in. Before I leave Capricorn I mean to kill him."

Melody's heart began a wild, frantic beating. "You'll never do it." But even as she said it, she was afraid for Flood.

Calloway's eyes turned ugly. His features

darkened. "He'll be dead in twenty-four hours, I tell you." His mouth twisted in the hard grin that had once intrigued her but which she now found frightening. "And you're going to help me kill him, Melody."

"No—no!" she protested. "I won't do it!"

"You'll help all right," he said. "Whether you want to or not!"

# Twenty-two

NELL and Flood had progressed two miles across the rolling tableland, bearing steadily away from the river, when they sighted two riders jogging toward them.

Flood pulled up instantly and sent a strident call through the night. "Raines, is that you?"

"Yeah, Dave!" came the Chevron owner's answering cry.

Immediately the speed of the riders increased. As they came nearer Flood noted that one of the horses was carrying double. At the same instant Raines made his own observation of Flood's gelding, and he shouted across the flats. "Have you got Nell with you, Dave?"

"Yeah. She's all right."

When Raines finally drew abreast of Flood and the girl he said, "God, Nell, I thought you'd gone down in that stampede. I lost sight of you once the critters started to run."

Pete Wendell was in the saddle behind Raines. Hoot Ellison rode the second horse. Ellison broke into the conversation before Nell could answer Raines. "How did you two meet up?"

"Just sheer luck," Flood said. "Nell got caught with a bunch that ran into that stretch of swamp where the river takes a wide bend."

"You mean you and your horse went into the mud?" Raines asked.

"Yes," Nell said, trembling at the memory of it. "And I never want to go through anything like it again. I'd almost rather be trampled underfoot. I imagine it's quicker and easier that way."

Raines slid a calloused hand over to Nell and took her wrist. "I'm sorry, Nell," he said with an odd tenderness. "It's my fault. I should never have let you come up here with us."

"Don't blame yourself," Nell told him. "I wanted to come and—after all—I didn't go down in the bog."

"It must have been close—too close." Raines looked at Flood.

"It was, Tom," Flood told him. "I heard the cattle on the move when I was a mile or two from the line shack. I just followed the dust trail. If I hadn't heard Nell scream—" He didn't finish. There was no need to go on. Every man there knew the slow and horrible death that the girl had just missed.

A brief silence settled over the group. Then Flood turned to Raines. "You figuring on trailing that beef tonight?"

"No, damn it!" growled Raines. "The bunch that rustled them kept a rear guard out. A couple of men with rifles holed up behind some rocks at the far end of the flats. They got Pete's horse and nearly winged me. We'll get after them in the morning. They're heading straight for the Tetons. It'll be slow going once they get in the high hills."

Flood nodded. "Here's something else, Tom. The bunch that hit the herd tonight were part of the same crowd that lifted the trail money from me in Blue Mesa."

A startled oath broke from Raines's throat. "Are you sure?"

"I ran into one of the bunch in town. He nearly drilled me with a .45 slug. He got away down an alley before I could get to him."

"But that's hardly proof that they're behind this raid."

"For me it is. Besides, Crandall, the new deputy, is one of the bunch too. In fact, Crandall is the fellow who ramrodded the whole operation in Blue Mesa. I got a description of him tonight from Marv Blackwell and I tell you it's the same man."

Then, while the others listened in stunned silence, Flood gave an account of Nap Rickard's attempt to kill him and his own subsequent talk with the sheriff.

"Tom," he said in conclusion, "Crandall and his pards are the men we want. My guess is that they mean to nail my hide to the wall and in the process they're out for a quick cleanup with stolen beef. Sam Hurst and his crowd are in the clear. If I can convince them that our hands are clean I'll ask them to join forces with us. We'll need every man we can spare if we have to comb the Tetons. It'll be bush war and not easy."

"Come on, then," said Raines. "Let's get back to the ranch. We'll have plenty to do between now and dawn. I'm getting those cow critters back if it's the last thing I ever do."

They pulled into the Chevron ranch yard an hour and a half later.

A light bloomed in the bunkhouse the moment they rode up to the corral. Val Evans, the puncher Raines had detailed for guard duty at the home ranch, ran outside.

"Melody with you?" the puncher called.

Raines's yell ripped right back at the man. "No, damn it! Isn't she here?"

"Nobody's been here since Kyle and Borden rode out to see about rounding up those cows you want driven up to Wind River."

Raines turned to Flood. "I don't like this, Dave," he said, and flung himself off his horse. He moved across the moon-dappled yard at a lumbering run and disappeared into the house.

The others had dismounted when Raines came out a few minutes later. A mixture of rage and fear contorted his face. "No sign of her inside," he announced. "Her bed hasn't been slept in." He looked from one to the other. "What do you make of it, Dave?"

"She might have decided to spend the night in

town," Flood said. But inside a sharp needle of worry began to stitch a cold seam up and down his spine. He was remembering Melody's flirtation with the deputy. It had concerned him before he realized the man's real identity. Knowing Calloway as he did—knowing the man was without scruples when it came to women— he wondered if the outlaw had simultaneously struck at him through Melody.

Meanwhile, Nell was talking to ease Raines's anxiety. "Tom, I don't think Melody liked the idea of being shut out tonight when you were making arrangements to guard the ranch and the cattle. She's bullheaded enough to go off to town because you ordered her to stay here."

"The damned fool!" growled Raines. "She never did have any sense. If she's in town I'm going in after her."

"I'll tag along, Tom," Flood said.

Raines snapped angrily at him. "I can handle my own wife without help."

"Sure you can," Flood agreed. "But I've got my reasons."

Raines's head jerked around. "You don't think Melody's fallen into the hands of that rustler bunch?"

"I didn't say that, but I'd like to go along."

Raines's cheeks turned gray and odd. He nodded dumbly and set about saddling a fresh horse for himself. Flood followed suit.

It was after midnight when Flood and Raines reached Capricorn. And within five minutes of their arrival they knew the worst. They found Melody's mare still tied to the hitch rack near the jail. Though they questioned the sleepy-eyed clerk in the hotel, woke up several storekeepers, and canvassed several saloons, asking everyone if they had seen her, they received the same negative answer.

"By God, they've got her!" raged Raines, stopping in front of the hotel with a knot of men, aroused by the fury of the search, gathered around him.

"It looks that way, Tom," Flood said.

"You want a posse, Raines?" someone yelled. "We'll get every manjack in this town that can ride a horse to help you find her."

"What's it all about?" the sleepy-eyed hotel clerk asked, pushing his way through the crowd.

"Never mind. Never mind," growled Raines. He shoved the men close to him roughly aside and strode to his horse. "Come on, Dave."

"What about a posse?" the man who had first made the suggestion called out.

"The Chevron takes care of its own," Raines snapped.

He heaved his big body into the saddle, waited for Flood to mount beside him. Then they spurred their mounts down the main street of Capricorn and headed back to the ranch. Once out of town

Raines turned to Flood. "How does it look to you?"

There was a tremulous roughness in Raines's words. The man was going through hell. He loved Melody in his own blundering, awkward way and the thought of her in the hands of a crew of cutthroats was driving him wild.

"Not good," Flood replied. "Crandall's got her. That's almost certain." Flood avoided using Calloway's real name lest his knowledge of it betray his own former closeness to the renegade. He added in a loud voice to carry over the rattle of their horses' hoofs, "Melody's horse being so close to the jail just about cinches it. None of her friends saw her. There's no place she could have gone we haven't checked."

Misery cut a wide, ragged track through Raines's talk. "But why, Dave? Why strike at Melody?"

Flood could think of one reason at once. Calloway was not above grabbing a woman he fancied—no matter whose brand she wore. He'd done it before, had bragged about it. And he'd taken a fancy to Melody. She, in turn, had welcomed his attentions.

But to Raines, Flood said, "Melody must have seen something in town tonight. Crandall and the jasper who tried to cash my chips had probably arranged to meet—maybe to talk over plans. They might have been in the sheriff's office or in back of some saloon. Wherever it was, Melody might have seen them together or overheard something that excited her suspicions about them."

"And they caught her at it," said Raines grimly.

"That's the only way I can figure it," Flood told him. "The damnable part of it is that Melody must have been here while I was in town. She may have even heard the shooting when I traded bullets with Crandall's friend. If I'd only seen her horse then."

The two men rode on for a half-mile in silence. Then Raines pushed his gelding close to Flood. "Dave," he said, "I'm going to get her back if I have to cover every foot of ground in the Tetons. And if Crandall and his bunch hurt her God help them because I'll kill every last one of them."

Flood, thinking of Calloway and Rickard and hating them for reasons of his own, added flatly: "If you don't, I will."

At two o'clock in the morning they rode into the Chevron ranch yard. Lamplight glimmered from the house and also from the windows of the bunkhouse. The sound of their horses brought Nell and the three Chevron punchers out into the yard.

"You didn't find her?" Nell asked incredulously.

"Her horse was there," said Raines, his features lined and gray with worry. "But no one had seen her."

"I can't understand it," said Nell. "What could have happened to her?" No one answered. Her eyes traveled from Raines's shocked features to the hard, bleak planes of Flood's face. Then a dread thought nagged at her brain. "You don't think Crandall could have anything to do with her disappearance?"

Nell had her answer in Flood's grim silent nod. "What will you do now?"

"We'll go after her," snapped Raines. "The cattle can go to blazes. It's Melody I want—and I won't stop riding till I get her back."

"But where will you look?"

"The Tetons."

"But there's miles and miles of hills and canyons up there."

"Don't you think I know that?" A hammering rage was working in Raines. It turned his talk rough and blunt. "I'll run every head of Chevron saddle stock into the ground but I'll find her." He waved an arm at Flood, Ellison, and the other two punchers. "Nothing we can do till daylight. Grab a couple of hours' sleep, then be ready to hit the saddle. And be sure that you pack plenty of .45 slugs for your guns. There are rifles in the house. We'll need them too."

"We're going to need more men, Tom," Flood said.

"No time for that now. A big crowd will slow us up."

"Sam Hurst will help if we go to him."

"I wouldn't ask him—not after what's happened between our two outfits the last few days."

"This is no time to be proud," Flood insisted. "And it is the time to straighten things out with Hurst." He swung his horse about. "You can stay here. I'm riding to the Sun. I'll be back by dawn." He saw red rage run its dark flux in Raines's cheeks, and he added quickly, "Don't try to stop me, Tom."

Flood swung away and started out of the yard. Then he heard a horse come clattering after him. Raines drew abreast. "All right," Raines said. "I'll go along."

They reached the Sun spread a little after three o'clock. It didn't take much to rouse the place. In a matter of minutes Sam Hurst was out in the yard, pulling a pair of jeans over his nightshirt. At the same time Mike Yorke and three Sun hands piled out of the bunkhouse.

Guns flared in the lamplight, Yorke's fighting yell cut through the night, and there was almost a clash of arms. But Raines's roaring shout brought silence. Quickly and bluntly he told Hurst and the others about Rickard's attempt to kill Flood and the simultaneous disappearance of Crandall and Melody.

"There it is, Sam," Raines said at last. "Things have busted wide open. The way we figure it is that Crandall's bunch has been chewing away at both of us. They got some of your beef last night. But I don't give a hoot for all the steers in Wyoming tonight. It's Melody I'm worried about. If you can spare a few men I'd be obliged to you."

Hurst's answer came without hesitation. "Every man here will ride with you, Tom. And that includes me. Just say the word."

Raines smiled bleakly. "Right now."

Hurst spoke to his crew. "Rattle your hocks, boys. We've some riding to do. And see to your hardware."

Mike Yorke glared at Flood, then turned away with the others. Flood realized the truce between them was only a temporary one. Yorke still wanted his revenge and he'd demand his chance. Flood regretted the ramrod's hatred but realized he could do nothing about it.

In twenty minutes the Sun riders were asaddle and ready for the trail. The party struck out at once with Raines and Flood at the head of the strung-out column.

Pale streaks of light were slashing through the dark eastern sky when they finally got back to the Chevron. And there a shocking surprise awaited them.

There were lights in the yard and men running back and forth. Nell ran up to Raines, who almost overran her with his gelding.

"We've heard from Melody!" Nell cried.

"What do you mean? Where is she?" Raines blurted.

"She's safe so far, I reckon," Hoot Ellison said. As Raines and Flood dismounted, Ellison handed the Chevron owner a large square of wrapping paper on which a crude message had been scrawled with a heavy black pencil.

The message read:

TOM RAINES,
    YOU CAN HAVE YOUR WIFE BACK ON ONE CONDITION. SEND DAVE FLOOD FOR HER. BUT HE'S GOT TO COME ALONE OR YOU'LL NEVER SEE HER AGAIN. IT'S UP TO YOU. FLOOD KNOWS WHERE TO LOOK.

The note was unsigned. Raines crumpled the paper in his rawhide fist. He glowered at Ellison. "Where did you find this?"

"Fastened to the bunkhouse door with a tack," Ellison said.

Raines choked up with rage. "The damn skunks were right here. In the last hour—while we were riding to the Sun ranch. By God, if I'd stayed we might have—" He broke off to ask another question: "Didn't you hear anything, Hoot?"

Ellison shook his head. "Whoever left that note was damned careful not to make any noise."

"Well, what are we waiting for?" demanded

Sam Hurst. "Let's head for the Tetons. If Flood here knows where to look we'll—"

Flood cut the Sun owner off. "No, Sam. That's the way to get Melody killed." Flood, at this moment, looked lean and tough and utterly cold. This was it. The call had gone out. His number had come up. He knew it and wanted them to know it. "This is aimed at me. Can't you see that?" He turned to Raines. "Crandall is ready to square accounts. He means to pull me in for a killing. And Melody's the bait."

"Hell, he won't get away with it!" Hurst roared.

"Yes, he will," said Flood. "I know Crandall. He's an Indian. He's got Melody. We can't take the chance of having her hurt. He's made the conditions. There's nothing else to be said." He moved past the tight, frozen group of men. "I'll need a fresh horse before I go," he said, and walked off toward the corral.

# Twenty-three

THE fierce, bright core of the day's heat lay like a suffocating weight upon Flood. He had been riding steadily for almost three hours and was now high in the Tetons. The country spread out before him, gashed and broken, forbidding and alone. The gray-blue sky, bare of clouds, had swallowed up the glaring white ball of the sun, blurring its edges.

A great weariness rode Flood's muscles, yet he sat stiff and straight in the saddle. There was a dreary cast to his craggy face. His narrowed eyes, squinting past the brim of his sombrero, held a raw, desolate look. He had the appearance of a man from whom all of life's vital juices had drained—a man whose horizons had closed down upon him.

Only a few miles separated him from the high mesa camp where he had surprised Calloway several months before. The string was running out fast. Automatically he swept his hand down to his Colt. He slid it in and out of the holster, thinking all the while what an empty gesture it was.

Behind him, an hour's ride away, was Tom Raines and the combined Chevron and Sun crews. He hadn't wanted them along. But Raines, almost out of his mind with worry and crowded by a headlong temper he'd never been able to restrain, had insisted he would take the risk of following Flood. His very insistence was an admission that he was aware Flood had started out on a one-way ride. If Melody failed to meet them along the backtrail within one hour after Flood reached the outlaw camp, Raines's plan was to attack the camp, regardless of consequences.

Ahead of Flood a brawling mountain brook spilled out of a narrow, high-walled defile. The water sped in a raging, foam-lashed torrent down its deep, rocky course, filling the air with the murmur of its passage. The trail swung into the canyon, following the stream. The thunder of the stream beat back and forth across the granite walls of the pass. The din of it pounded Flood's ears. He welcomed the coolness of the canyon, but the respite was of short duration, for the trail soon fell out of the defile and wandered across an open bench where the sun once again hit him with its down-pressing ceiling of heat.

At the end of another mile the bench skirted a low line of ruby-colored bluffs. Beyond the bluffs the trail pitched upward toward a thickly wooded ridge. Just as Flood cantered past the rock wall Nap Rickard rode across the trail, his gun swinging down on Flood.

"So you walked right into Calloway's trap," Rickard said as Flood raised his hands.

Flood's features did not change. His eyes, resting on Rickard's taut shape, were flinty and unafraid. "You knew I would," he said.

Rickard rode carefully around Flood, then came up behind him and lifted his gun out of the holster. He swung back alongside of Flood. He thrust Flood's weapon into the waistband of his levis. "I reckon I don't have to tell you that you won't be riding out again," he murmured, an odd relish for the situation putting a greedy shine in his eyes.

Rickard's voice was gentle. He was as close to smiling as Flood had ever seen him. He might have been passing the time of day instead of telling Flood he was going to die.

A violent instinct stirred Flood's lips, but he said nothing. His cheeks grew stony. There was a cold, almost frightening detachment about him. He had no fear of death. The close, hard risks of his life in this rugged land where only the strong could make a firm place for themselves had inured him to the thought of death.

He had only one regret—that he probably wouldn't see Nell again. The thought of her now was like a hard ball bouncing around his insides. He remembered with terrible clarity how Nell had come to him at the corral before he rode away from the Chevron ranch.

She had flung her arms around him, pulled his mouth down to hers, and kissed him with a wild, sweet abandon. She had been all passion and ardor, her supple body pressing against him in a furious, hungry seeking. It was as if, knowing she soon would have no more of him, she had to have all of him for the few minutes of time that was left to her.

When she freed her mouth at last Flood found her looking at him with eyes that were fever-bright and close to tears. At that moment she was the loveliest woman he had ever seen. He saw she was fighting panic.

She didn't ask him not to go because she knew it was something he had to do. There could be no changing that. It was part of the creed men lived by in this untamed, sometimes heartless country. All she said was, "I'll be waiting for you, Dave."

Then she turned and ran off toward the Chevron ranch house. Afterward, Raines and the others crowded around him to watch him mount and ride away toward the Tetons.

Now, with Rickard silently and mockingly watching him, Flood said with a sudden savage insistence, "Let's get on with it."

"Sure," said the outlaw. "You know the way, so you can ride ahead. And remember if you make a break I'll put a bullet in your back."

"There'll be no break," said Flood as he rode on out ahead. "Calloway's the man I want to see."

Half an hour later they came to the high, boulder-strewn bench which served Calloway for a camp. They climbed the steep, juniper-dotted slope to the flat shelf of land. Then they skirted the rambling wall of rocks, cut into the narrow gap, and rode into the open glade.

Calloway was waiting, gun in hand. He had seen them when they first started up the grade. Now his harsh, triumphant voice cut at Flood like a whip. "I've been waiting a long time for this, Flood."

Flood gave him a hard look, then turned to Melody, who had risen from a blanket tossed down on the ground near the ashes of a fire. She was pale and worried, but her face brightened when she saw Flood.

"Dave! Oh, Dave, I'm glad you've come." She started toward him, but Calloway waved her back. "Where's Tom and the others?"

"I came alone, Melody," Flood told her.

Her cheeks looked suddenly stricken. "But you must have known—Crandall told me that he was—" She stopped in confusion and terror.

"I know, Melody," Flood said quietly.

"Dave!" she burst out. "They're going to kill you!"

"I know that too."

"No!" The word was a scream. She raced toward Flood. Calloway stepped in front of her, caught her with one hand and flung her roughly to the ground.

"Calloway!" Flood's fists bunched and he

lunged forward. But Rickard followed and rammed his gun barrel into Flood's back.

Calloway swung around, wickedly grinning. "You've still got a soft spot when it comes to women, my friend."

"Don't put your hands on her again, Bill, or you'll have to kill me right now," Flood told him grimly.

"I never saw a man so anxious to die," said Calloway, hefting the heavy Colt in his fist. "The rest of the boys ought to be here to see your finish. Too bad they're busy hazing that Chevron beef toward Idaho."

Melody got slowly to her feet. Despair held her in an implacable grip. There was no life in her, no hope. Her eyes seemed to be out of focus and she couldn't stop the hysterical quivering of her mouth.

"All right, Bill," Flood said. "I've kept my side of our bargain. Give Melody her horse and start her off for home."

"Later, my friend."

"Start her now, Bill." Flood's words were low and deadly. A savage, inflexible wildness was prodding him.

"No," said Calloway. "I figured she might like to watch the show."

All of Calloway's wickedness showed in his talk. He had set himself for the kill, but the insane cruelty that was in him wanted more than Flood's death. He wanted Flood to crawl, wanted him to suffer. But Flood wasn't a man to crawl, so he had to strike through Melody once again.

Flood moved toward Calloway. He saw suddenly that he'd been a complete fool. Calloway had no intention of letting Melody go. He'd used her as bait to pull him—Flood—into a death trap. Now he'd kill and move on with the girl. And when he was finished with Melody no man would want her.

"Start shooting, Bill," Flood droned, "before I kill you with my bare hands."

Calloway retreated, his gun level. He continued to grin. "We'll do this my way. I'm going to give you a chance to run." He pointed to the tumbled stand of rocks a hundred yards away. "If you reach those rocks before I count to three you can take your chances against Nap and me."

Flood stared at the tumbled mass of boulders. Directly within line of them were the gray-black ashes of the campfire. A heavy metal coffeepot rested in the ashes. Rickard stood to the right of the fire, watching Flood with a nervous, bleak attention. Calloway was to the left of the fire. Beyond and a little behind Calloway stood Melody. Her face now was a white mask of fear in which her eyes looked like pitted coals.

A reckless stir of excitement washed across Flood's features. His eyes had a curious, far-reaching expression in them. He said, "Suppose I don't run?"

Calloway shrugged carelessly. "That's up to you. One!"

"Dave!" The cry was torn from Melody's throat.

But Flood didn't hear it. As if his long, lean body were propelled by a steel spring, he shot forward and away from Calloway. The outlaw's deep-toned "Two!" rang out as Flood reached the campfire ashes. He stopped in mid-stride, bent to the blackened coals, and grabbed the soot-smeared handle of the coffeepot. In almost the same motion he wheeled up and around, his arm cocking backward for a throw at Calloway.

He was dimly aware of Rickard's warning shout. Then Flood lost his target when Melody flung herself upon Calloway, her hands slashing at his gun arm.

Rickard fired as Flood wheeled half around again. The bullet burned a hot track along the top of his left shoulder. Pain was a leaping flare of agony traveling down the length of Flood's arm. But he hurled the coffeepot straight at Rickard and followed it at a low, crouching run.

Rickard's gun blasted once more. Then he went down as the metal coffeepot struck him high on the forehead. He hit the earth flat on his back and didn't move after that. Flood's lunge carried him in a flat dive toward Rickard. He skidded along the ground on his chest, taking a terrific jar in his shoulder that almost made him black out. He got his fingers on Rickard's gun and heard Melody's hurt cry as Calloway smashed her to the ground with a sharp, chopping blow to the point of her chin.

"Three!" Calloway roared, and fired his piece.

But Flood's shot came a split second ahead of the renegade's. A puff of dust spiraled away from Calloway's shirt front, showing where Flood's slug had found its mark. Simultaneously a bullet kicked up a spray of dirt in Flood's eyes where he lay prone beside Rickard. Flood pawed at his eyes to clear his vision, centered his sights on Calloway for a follow-up, then let the barrel of Rickard's Colt sag.

A look of blind, gray shock filled Calloway's face. Wind rushed out of his lungs and through his slack splayed mouth. Then his body jerked in spastic convulsions, his eyes rolled crazily in his head, and he pitched woodenly forward.

Sunset found Flood, Melody, and Tom Raines within a mile of the Chevron ranch house. Behind them lay the many miles of broken, rutted country that made up the Teton range. And behind them also lay the memory of a bitter fight that was now over.

For a few minutes after Calloway fell dead under Flood's single bullet Melody had been hysterical. The strain of her ordeal had beaten down all her defenses. She had been like a child, alone and afraid of the dark. She had clung to Flood until, finally, he had broken her hold and slapped her face. The blow startled her and angered her, but it shocked her back to sensibility.

Once in control of her feelings Melody had insisted on bandaging Flood's shoulder wound which proved to be only a shallow furrow. Then Flood had gotten the horses. He had lifted Calloway's body into the saddle, tied it fast. Afterward he ordered Rickard aboard a second horse and lashed his ankles under the animal's belly.

Leaving the outlaw camp, they negotiated the treacherous slope and continued along the winding back trail, meeting Raines's party a mile beyond the high-walled canyon that carried the brawling, unnamed mountain stream. Two men had been detached from the group to take Rickard and Calloway into Capricorn. The remainder, led by Hoot Ellison and Sam Hurst, went on deeper into the Tetons to get the stolen cattle and round up Calloway's hired gun-slicks. Rickard, all the fight gone out of him, had painted a clear picture of where Hurst's men could expect to come upon their steers.

Now, as Flood, Raines, and Melody drew close to Chevron headquarters, Flood noted with an odd sense of wonderment how Melody's terrifying experience had drawn her closer to Raines. Some of her hard surface veneer had been chipped away. She seemed chastened and serene. Watching her, Flood saw a strange tenderness in her eyes when she glanced at Raines.

When they rode into the ranch yard Nell was waiting for them. She came running to meet Flood. He barely had time to swing down from his horse before she was in his arms. "Oh, Dave!" she said, half-laughing and half-crying. "I—I can hardly believe you're back. I—I was afraid to hope." She kissed him, her mouth warm and moist and full of surrender.

After a moment she drew away and hurried to Melody and hugged the other girl to her. "Melody, you're all right."

"Yes, thanks to Dave," said Melody. "Nell, you'll never know how close a thing it was."

Flood had his head turned to regard Melody and Nell when he saw a tall, dark figure move out of the shadows of the veranda. Syd Stack, sheriff of Blue Mesa, came down the steps and approached Flood.

Raines bellowed his surprise. "What brings you out this way, Syd?" the rancher demanded.

"You've come to see me?" Flood cut in.

Stack nodded, taking a much-folded sheet of glossy paper out of his shirt pocket.

"I've been expecting you, Syd," Flood said.

"What's it all about?" demanded Raines.

Nell looked suddenly worried. A dark frown gathered on Raines's deeply tanned forehead.

"I reckon it's a private matter, Tom," the sheriff replied.

"They might as well hear it," said Flood, a note of resignation in his voice. He flashed a glance at Nell, pleading for understanding. He added gently, "I've been living on borrowed time. Time borrowed from Yuma Prison in Arizona."

Nell's smooth, round face registered shock. "Dave, you don't know what you're saying."

"I'm afraid I do." He gestured to the folded paper in Stack's fist. "The sheriff's got a reward dodger there in his hand. It probably has my picture on it."

"But Dave, I don't understand."

"It's simple enough," he said. "I knew Calloway—whom you all knew as Crandall—much better than anyone realized. He and his pards saved my life one time when I was down on my luck. Afterward I fell in with them even though I soon figured they were riding the owl hoot." He paused briefly, then went on to review his early association with Calloway which terminated in the abortive bank holdup, their arrest, their stay in prison and subsequent escape. "I'm sort of glad it's all over now," he concluded. "I'm ready to go back with you, Syd."

The sheriff's worn, weather-seamed face was suddenly grave and intent. "I heard from Nell the job you undertook," he said. "There aren't many men I know who would have taken the risk you took and fewer who could live to talk about it. You got Calloway?"

"Yeah," Flood replied somberly. "Calloway's dead and Rickard's on his way to the calaboose in Capricorn. They're the only ones you're interested in, Syd."

Stack nodded. Admiration for the big, hard-visaged Chevron ramrod showed in his direct glance. "You've just about wiped the slate clean."

"Hell," said Raines, "then tear up that reward poster and go back to Blue Mesa. Dave's not the first hombre to make a slip. And he's paid it all back."

"Everything you say is true, Tom," the sheriff admitted. "But the law is technical. Dave's got to go back to Yuma." He lifted a hand when he saw an angry tide of blood flush upward into Raines's neck and face. "Hold it," said Stack. "Sure it sounds silly, but it's got to be done. But I can promise you this. I'll wire the governor of Arizona all the facts in the case. I'm sure when the information is before him he'll grant Dave a full pardon."

"But that might be months from now," protested Raines.

"It might be a few weeks or, at the most, two or three months."

Flood turned away, no longer caring what Raines and Stack said to each other. He had eyes only for Nell. He approached her, his glance searching her face. "Nell, I'm sorry about this," he murmured.

She smiled then. It was like a ray of light splashing upon her cheeks. The light was in her eyes too. It warmed Flood, pulled him near. She put her arms around him and suddenly all the fierce, pent-up need for her was like a bolt of living flame shooting through him.

"Did you think it would make any difference, Dave?" she asked.

He didn't answer. He just looked at her, marveling at her loveliness and at the naked desire that burned in her eyes. She pulled his face down to hers. When she kissed him, her eager lips told him that all of her gifts were his for the taking.

"Two weeks—two months—even if it were two years," she murmured, "I'd still be waiting here for you."

**Center Point Large Print**
600 Brooks Road / PO Box 1
Thorndike ME 04986-0001 USA

(207) 568-3717

US & Canada:
1 800 929-9108
www.centerpointlargeprint.com